CU00866934

Beautifully Mundane

Chris Barton

Copyright © 2014 Chris Barton

All rights reserved, including the right to reproduce this book, or portions thereof in any form. No part of this text may be reproduced, transmitted, downloaded, decompiled, reverse engineered, or stored, in any form or introduced into any information storage and retrieval system, in any form or by any means, whether electronic or mechanical without the express written permission of the author.

This is a work of fiction. Names and characters are the product of the author's imagination and any resemblance to actual persons, living or dead, is entirely coincidental.

ISBN: 978-1-291-76667-7

PublishNation, London

www.publishnation.co.uk

To The Bevingtons

Chapter One

As he tried to feel for the pen which had managed to roll under the desk, just tantalisingly out of reach of his outstretched fingers, David started to wonder about the peculiarity of life. Why me? Why me? Everybody asks it, nobody has an answer because of the rhetorical nature of the question. You would be better off asking why not me to which any answer is just as insanely plausible. At times like this as his head reeled with the day to day mundanities of everyday living, what bill should I pay first, when is the right time to replace the broken cooker, why is that car so expensive, that David always felt envious of those people who find a kooky religion, and have that weird smile with the glazed over eyes. "Yes we believe that the alien prophet Zandru will one day return to the planet Earth and release us from the torments that make us human, and through his appointee to this world, Lord Kllaxu, whose earthly name is John Petterson, and for just a small percentage of our wages, he can guide us so we will be ready for his return." It always seemed to David that Lord Kllaxu's nearest and dearest devotees were good looking young girls who, despite their reservations, had to give themselves over to this messiah for fear of upsetting their 'new family', or the sinister looking henchmen at his side. At least they are happy David thought to himself.

"What are you doing?" Andrew Smith, fellow employee, boss and occasional right pain in the posterior.

"I am trying to get my pen out from under the desk, it's got stuck near the legs and I can't quite reach it."

"Well don't, Dixon is going to be here in a minute and the last thing he wants to see is is you scrabbling about on the floor."

Ah yes, Graeme Dixon area manager for region 28, and Andrew Smith's version of Kllaxu for the Harman and Cooke Insurance Agency. To Smith's way of thinking Graeme Dixon was on 35k a year plus bonuses and that put him next to the Gods. The actual

Gods being the board of Directors for the insurance agency, allowing for the fact that neither Mr Harman nor Mr Cooke were still alive, if indeed they ever existed in the first place.

About two years ago those same board of Directors, in their infinite wisdom, decided to send the region 28 staff away for the weekend on a team building exercise in the country, otherwise known to David Banks as the worst days of his life. It is one thing to be stuck in the woods with a load of strangers on a miserable Saturday afternoon, but even worse to realise that you have nothing in common with them at all. Most of them seemed to communicate through sport, "Did you see the game on Wednesday? What do you think his chances are of making it through to the final? Who do you fancy for the cup?" These low points in Hell were nothing compared to the ultimate nadir of suddenly realising that you and the area manager for region 28, Andrew's messiah, are in fact polar opposites. David hated golf, a sport he knew nothing about, or ever wanted to. George Dixon was Mr Golf, his sole reason for living as it turned out, a fact that never passed Andrew by as he went straight out and enrolled for his local golf club the following week. David took consolation in the fact that no matter how hard he tried, and he did try, Andrew was the worst golfer that ever took the fairways of any golfing green since golf was invented. When the weekend was over everybody shook hands and prayed to God inside that they would never have to do this ever again. So far their wishes had come true.

"Here he comes now, act natural," hissed Andrew. What other way was there to act?

"Good morning team." Dixon strolled into the office with the confidence of a man who long ago had decided he was right about everything, and if only the rest of the world would do things his way everything would be fine. This from the man whose wife still ironed his socks.

So here they were gathered together around the right Reverend Graeme Dixon, Harman and Cooke's finest insurance claim checkers region 28 had to offer. David scanned them as they clustered together around the office, my fellow workers, my compatriots, my gang. Firstly there was Felicity, mid thirties, overweight, single, plain looking, good at her job. Some obese girls could look quite stunning if they lost a few stone, but alas David felt that for poor Felicity this would never be the case. Despite this she had still managed to pull quite a few boyfriends over the years, much to everyone's surprise. Several years ago she had lost a baby but that was a subject that nobody would ever dare broach. Then there was Adam, the new boy, not yet 21, dumb yet likable, he could be relied upon to get coffee and the occasional discourses about cars and girls, subjects to which Adam was very well informed. Everybody in the office was jealous of the fact that Adam had joined too late to go on the bonding weekend, and therefore had never been stuck in a freezing cold river with bits of twig lapping around his waist. Some liked his blonde hair. Next in line was Eric, the ghost of Adam future, a thirty something go-getter who was always on the lookout for some get rich quick scheme that was going to make him millions, and which never seemed to materialise. If there was an award for how many times a day a man could check himself in the mirror then Eric would get it. He was always going on about his near conquests with girls, "the ladies," but everyone knew he would never leave his long suffering mousey girlfriend Lolita. After Eric was the old man of the group, Ronald, sad but sweet, once upon a time he had been very wealthy and had gone quite far up the company ladder, but some major disagreement with the top echelons, and more than just a few major financial misjudgements, had led him to virtual bankruptcy and a demotion to region 28. Eric and Andrew avoided Ronald like the plague, as though mere association could contaminate them and destroy their plans to make it to the top. David liked him. David liked him a lot. Last in line, apart from David himself, was Andrew, married father of one, a man who had managed thus far to ingratiate his way up the career ladder, and, being in his late forties, would probably find this meteoric rise was waning in its ascendancy. One day Andrew would retire, and reflect on those heady days when he basked in the glory of the Harman and Cooke Insurance Agency.

"...and I can therefore report that we are up 6% on last years targets, but we are down on our goals for the next fiscal year," Dixon droned on, "but with internet sales improving, and our new three for two policy, we can make net gains throughout the industry as a whole. Thanks for listening."

Silence. Deafening silence, was he really expecting a round of applause? "Well thank you Graeme that was great and I think that we should all put our hands together in appreciation of that fine speech." Well done Andrew always able to make a calamity out of a crisis. The excruciatingly muted round of smattered applause which followed would have embarrassed the Devil.

Nonplussed and confidant in his superiority, Dixon stumbled on, "Does anybody have any questions?" he asked.

David had no questions, in fact, he had spent most of the oration trying desperately to get the Pink Panther theme music out of his head. More awkward silence. "I have a question," God bless you Andrew, at times even the obsequious have their uses. "What percentage of sales can be attributed to the discount we offer for any customer who buys three or more insurance products?" Everybody knew that Andrew already knew the answer. Was there anything he did not know about the company, he practically slept with the bi-annual report under his pillow, but they were all grateful for this interjection, even Dixon. Dixon probably was also aware of the fact that Andrew knew the answer, too, but as a drowning man will grab at anything which floats past he rolled with it. "Well I am very glad that you asked that question, Andrew, as I am pleased to report that in the few short months we have been running this scheme, we have seen sales in this area practically triple, bucking the trend of a downturn in the multiple policy sales area generally."

"I have a question," all eyes turned to Adam, incredulous, "What time are we going to break up for dinner?" The innocence of youth. Silence again, this day would go down in history. And then Dixon laughed, and then Andrew laughed, and then everybody laughed, not because it was funny but because they were all caught in a moment. "Young man," said Dixon, "That is a very good idea, let's go now."

4

After dinner the mood in the office was much more light-hearted. Dixon had gone to assert his reverence somewhere else, and the general atmosphere was that of a group of people who had survived a near miss, and were in the motorway cafe laughing about it afterwards. "I wonder what Mrs Dixon looks like," Eric surmised, "Do you think that they ever have sex?" You could always rely on Eric to bring the conversation to a new low. After a few celebratory cups of coffee and a packet of digestives, the team went back to their work.

Sometimes there is comfort to be had in the mundane humdrum of everyday office life, safe, boring, comforting, everybody knew their place, David almost felt contented.

Chapter Two

After work David went home. "You wouldn't believe the kind of day I've had," he said to no-one in particular as he walked through the door. His wife Jessica was in the kitchen. Jessica and David had been childhood sweethearts, from when they had met at the after school disco. No hearts and flowers and wild romance for these two. When all of their friends had paired off with each other for various dances, the two had found themselves staring at each other, awkward and embarrassed, neither daring to say anything to the other. "Well, we had better go out then," Jessica had declared and they had ever since. Over the years David had realised that he loved her more and more, to the point where he now thought God knows what he would do without her. It really pleased David that while they had watched all of their other school friend's relationships fizzle out and die, theirs had stayed strong.

What was that smell? Freshly baked carrot cake, David's favourite, and if his olfactory senses were not mistaken was that not a roast in the oven, and on a Tuesday. He flung open the kitchen door like a gunslinger walking into the saloon to find the varmint who had shot his son. "When is she coming?" he demanded.

"Hello dear, did the office visit go alright?" asked Jessica.

"Don't pretend not to hear me, when is she coming and for how long?" They both knew what he was talking about, to most people the dreaded mother in law was just a cliché the stuff of comic books, and low rent sit coms, but to David the reality was even worse. Jessica's parents had set their hearts on the fact that one day their precious, and only daughter, would marry a high flying lawyer from the city, or a rich banker, or they even dared hope, nobility. Instead they got David the spotty, long-haired (at that time), layabout (in their opinion) who was good for nothing. "It killed your father" Jessica's mother loved to say. Not the bowel cancer, David secretly thought, just lately he had even started to wonder if she had poisoned

6

the poor henpecked sod. David repeated the question, "I said, when is she coming and for how long?"

Well it's only for a few days, just until her leg gets better after the operation," Jessica said defensively.

David could feel his heart icing up, he felt genuine fear. "Days...operation..." his mind started to reel good God in Heaven she could mean months. He tried to hold on to the fact that even with modern medicine people still die under anaesthetic.

"You know I told you she is going in for surgery on her knee, we cannot just leave her to struggle around in her house on her own."

"Yes we can."

"After all the house is fifty miles away.."

"Not far enough."

"...and she is almost sixty-five."

That last remark put in to make David feel guilty, the secret message being that Jessica had already lost one parent and was not ready to lose another. To David losing another was a beacon of hope.

"Besides the children love her, it would do them good to spend some time with their grandmother."

The children were completely indifferent to their grandmother and saw her only as a source of extra income. In turn 'granny' doted on them and saw David's part in their creation as a genetic flaw, a virus that given enough love and time could be eliminated out of them.

"So when is she coming?" David lowered his voice.

"Saturday week if all goes well."

Saturday week, but that only gives me eleven days to mentally prepare, David's mind went back into overdrive mode. He reached for the carrot cake. "You cannot have that now," said Jessica, "tea will be ready in half an hour." This day was turning out to be the best.

David went into the living room to wait for his supper and watch a bit of television to keep his mind occupied, the kids were upstairs, he put his feet on the coffee table and tried to enjoy the eleven days of freedom he had left. Normally quiz shows entertained him but not today, he could not hear any of the questions without envisaging the looming spectre of the black widow leering over him. Jessica brought in dinner, the kids had already eaten theirs earlier. Sometimes David wondered if he and Jessica ever had children. The news had just started. "The Chancellor has publicly stated that the economic downturn is set to get worse," announced the presenter, forgetting to add, "By the way your mother in law is coming," in David's mind. Five minutes of boring statistics later, in which everyone from the cub reporter upwards declared the country all but bankrupt, and at last they were on to the second story. "The second story was a harrowing report from some war torn country on the other side of the world, where the refugees had gone without food and water for days on end, with equally graphic images to match. "How is your tea, David?" the imaginary voice of the newsreader continued, "Those roast potatoes still tasting good, and don't forget the mother in law will be here within days." The next story was about a madman running around the streets of London with an axe. At last, thought David, something good, something interesting. The news ended with some pensioners waving from the royal balcony, and the whole world was a nice place again, apart from the commoners who had to live in it.

"Where is your mother going to sleep?" David turned to his wife, "She can't sleep in Lucy's room and Simon's room is full of crap," by which he meant technology.

"She is going to have to sleep on the sofa bed down here, besides she wouldn't be able to get up the stairs," Jessica replied.

"Oh" he had no feelings on the matter, the fact that the Gorgon had already got through the door would be enough. Where she made her lair was of no importance to him.

Later as they were doing the dishes together, which involved David loading the dishwasher and Jessica making cups of tea, it suddenly dawned on him that he might be able to turn this situation to his advantage. With careful planning and the right words dropped into the right conversation, in the right place, he might be able to convince Jessica to let him have the new television he had been pining after. Vive la electronique revolution!!

8

The kitchen door burst open, it was surely getting a pounding today, and their eldest child Lucy stormed in. Somewhere between innocent childhood and those delicate teenage years she had discovered Goth, which for her was less of a lifestyle choice and more of a religion. David hated it, even worse he could not bring himself to admit he hated it. No dance rehearsals or fairytale prom night dress for this distraught father. To think that he had cried at the birth.

"Mary Parker says that she and some of the other girls are going on a skiing holiday with the school this summer, it's all over Facebook" Lucy declared. God bless the internet, thought David, sometimes he wondered how any of the kids communicated with each other before the dawn of computing.

"Would you like to go with them, dear?" Jessica responded.

. Where did that come from? David liked it, well done Jessica, he decided to hitch his wagon to the same star. "We have been putting some money aside for your college fund," David said to his daughter, "Maybe we could dip into it a little, and you could go with them."

"You'd like that wouldn't you..."Lucy screamed, storming out of the kitchen in the same frenzied manner as she had arrived. Who could understand the teenage mind? Not Jessica, not David, they stared at each other in stunned silence as they each tried to analyse what the Hell just happened.

"I'll talk to her later," Jessica finally decided, and there the matter was laid to rest.

Inspired by the total communications breakdown with his daughter, David decided to pay a visit to the only other occupant of the house, apart from a stray cat who had adopted them, his eleven year old son, Simon. Most parents dream of having a highly intelligent gifted child, that would one day go on to do genius things with pipe smoking scholarly types, but to David it was a curse. He had wanted a son who might do better than ogling over pictures in lads magazines, and admiring super rich footballers, but maybe Simon had gone too far into the void. It certainly made for difficult conversations when your son was more interested in the dense molecular structure of lead than motor racing. Still he had to keep

9

trying, even if it did make him feel uncomfortable, perhaps Simon would turn out to be gay, after all nature has a subtle way of balancing these things out in the wash.

He knocked timidly on the bedroom door. He took the muted grunt from the interior of the room do be a sign for entry. "Hello Simon, did you have a nice day at school?" it sounded trite. He glanced around at all of the electrical items cluttering up what was once a decent size box room. Computers, monitors, games stations, mobile devices, tablets, wires, so many wires, does any world need this many wires.

"Nah not really," Simon responded.

"Oh, that's nice...what you reading?"

"Well actually dad it's a pamphlet my chemistry teacher gave me on the photo-synthetic properties of certain plants, and how they responded to different sections of the light spectrum. I have to say it is very interesting." David's heart sank, he wanted to feel the love, he really did, even if he wanted to feign interest he knew so little about the subject that he did not have a clue where to begin.

"Sounds great," he lied, "Did you know that your sister was thinking of going on a skiing holiday this summer? Would you like to do anything like that?"

"Not really, sounds a bit 'trick' if you ask me." What the Hell was 'trick'? He had heard it used several times, the latest buzz word from America that meant nothing, and everything, or whatever it was that you supposed it to mean.

"OK but if you change your mind be sure to let me or your mother know."

"Sure thing, dad."

Disheartened David skulked his way back downstairs.

Chapter Three

The next morning in the office Felicity was crying. At first everyone pretended not to notice but when a few silent tears turned into uncontrollable sobs, David felt that maybe he ought to intervene. "Is everything alright, Felicity?" he asked cautiously. Clearly everything was not alright, maybe she had lost another baby, she had not looked pregnant but it was hard to tell these days what with the weight problem, and well you never know. Maybe it was the anniversary of the baby's death, women can be so peculiar about these things, he hoped it had nothing to do with babies.

"My little fluffykins died this morning," she blurted out in wails of sobs.

Fluffykins, fluffykins...that sure was an unusual name to call a baby. Perhaps her sad loss affected her mind more than anyone thought.

"I woke up this morning and there she was curled up in her little basket...I thought that she was asleep but she was dead..." more sobs, louder now.

The realisation that she was talking about one of her cats, and not a dead baby of any sort, flooded David with relief. Oh thank God, he almost blurted out just managing to stop himself in the nick of time. He tried to think of a response, something comforting, something positive, "Maybe it was her time and she has gone to a better place," he offered.

"But she was only four years old, and she had a lovely fluffy tail like no other cat and I really, really loved her." Felicity continued her mournful rail between wailing.

Quite difficult to follow that one, thought David, pondering for a moment.

Eric tried to help, "Cheer up Felicity...after all it's only an animal it is not like you have lost a baby or anything." Well done Eric, in one single sentence you have managed to turn a difficult situation into the most awkward embarrassing moment on earth. Shocked silence followed in which everyone glared at Eric. "Well I was just saying," Eric stumbled on, desperately looking around him for some clemency in the eyes of the angry onlookers. Even Adam gave him disapproving looks.

The only sound to cut the atmosphere, and oh boy you really could cut the atmosphere, was Felicity's sobs. David put his hand on her shoulder unsure of the right thing to do, this office needs another woman, he thought, I am sure another female would know what to do.

"I remember when I lost my dog," Ronnie broke the silence, "When was it now, twenty, twenty-five years ago...it was a bit like losing an arm." Normally David did not like Ronald's nostalgic monologues, because as everybody in the office was painfully aware they could have a tendency to go on and on, but today David was prepared to relish every word that came out of his mouth. "I remember that it was a lovely sunny day and I had just come back from fishing, usually my Fido would rush out to greet me, she loved the smell of fish, she was a red setter you know..."

Andrew opted for a timely interruption, "Felicity, would you like to have the rest of the day off? Maybe you could go home and rest, it might help you to feel better." David could not decide whether this offer was prompted by compassion or necessity, on the grounds that the rest of the staff would be able to carry on with their work without this disruption. Knowing Andrew like he did he went for the latter. Nothing was said.

"That is very kind of you Andrew, very kind indeed, but I have so many claims to work on I am not sure I would be able to catch up..."said Felicity, still sobbing but more muted now.

"Nonsense, David can help you, and so will Eric and Adam..." Thanks Andrew as if I have not got a heavy enough work load as it is, thought David to himself, knowing that Eric and Adam would probably be more of a hindrance than a help. Why not Ronnie, David thought, Andrew never asked Ronnie. "Besides," Andrew continued, "you shouldn't be trying to work with all of this distress."

"That would be lovely, Andrew," said Felicity, "I could go home and try to sort out the funeral with the cats parlour." Maybe you could bury it next to your baby. David instantly admonished himself for having such dark thoughts.

Everybody sheepishly busied themselves at their desks and tried to avoid eye contact, as Felicity quietly gathered her things and got her scarf and coat. "I am off now," she said to the room in general, and then added the word, "Thanks," as she walked out the door. After she had gone there was a pregnant silence for a while, until Andrew called across to David to ask if he had some of the back files relating to flood damage in the Loughborough area. Whether it was a tension relief thing, or the way he said it, or the unreality of the whole situation, or for some God knows what reason, David thought this was the funniest thing on earth. At first he tried to suppress it but the feeling just got stronger and stronger, and before long it just had to come out. He started to laugh, and then he nearly pissed himself, the others started laughing too, and within moments everybody was practically rolling about on the floor wiping the tears from their eyes and holding their sides with laughter. At this point Felicity walked back into the office. The look of confusion and bewilderment on her face could have painted a thousand pictures. "I forgot to give you back the keys to the filing cabinets," she said directly to Andrew, who at this moment was a small boy of three years old, stark naked, with his hand inside the cookie jar.

"Thank you," Andrew squeaked, as he limp wristedly accepted the bunch of keys from her outstretched hands. Everybody in the office had now died!

"Well I'm off now," Felicity said to the morgue, as she turned on her heels and went.

Mortified, the remaining staff of Harman and Cooke Insurance Agency, region 28 claim checking department, stared at each other as if they had just seen a ghost. After a while, Adam ventured to end their discomfort by turning to Eric and asking the age old question, "Did you see the football last night?" Well done Adam, if any situation is steeped in uncertainty it is always best to find the lowest common denominator, and that can only be sport, genius choice.

13

The whole office agreed that if that goal had not been disallowed, by a referee who was patently blind, they would have won.

David kicked back on his swivel chair, safe in the knowledge that things were returning to normal. He wondered if at some point if he, or some poor unfortunate nominee, usually Andrew, ought to telephone Felicity to see if she was feeling any better. He floated the idea with the rest of the staff but it was decided by mutual consent that they might make a difficult situation even worse. Sometimes it is hard to know how to do the right thing. Ronald suggested that they all club together and buy her a bunch of flowers, for when she came back to work, and everybody thought this was a marvellous idea, less on the grounds that it was the right thing to do, and more perhaps that each and every one of them was feeling guilty inside. A whip round was had, and Adam was promptly dispatched.

"What sort of flowers?" Adam decried.

"Any..." seemed to be the response from the general consensus.

After a while Adam came back with the most wilted, sorrowful looking bunch of flowers ever to leave a supermarket shelf. Never send a boy to do a man's job, thought David.

"Did you get a card to go with them?" asked Andrew.

"What card? Nobody told me that I had to get a card." Adam replied.

Adam was once more sent into the breach, this time under strict instructions to return the flowers, and get a better bunch, and also to get a card. An hour later he returned with another bunch of flowers, only slightly improved on the previous one, and a card. The front of the card read...'With Deepest Sympathy' inside did not get any better...'Just to let you know that our thoughts and feelings are with you at this time.' "Is that the best card they had?" Andrew felt the need to enquire.

Adam surely felt persecuted today, "Well I didn't know what sort of card to get, there was loads," he bleated.

"Never mind this one will have to do," said Andrew.

Dutifully one by one they all signed the card. When it was David's turn he was glad to note that at least there was no reference to dead babies, of any sort, neither in the wording or the pictures. If any of the others had noticed this, they simply did not say. The flowers were placed on Felicity's desk where they could wilt some more, and the card put next to them. The hope was that she would find them in the morning and her forgiveness would be absolute.

Later on everybody went home.

Chapter Four

Over the next few days David's apprehension grew worse and worse. Even the children, having grilled their mother for every last detail about the imminent arrival of their grandmother, turned their Gestapo techniques upon their father.

"How long is she going to be staying for, dad?"

"I don't know."

"What sort of operation is she having?"

"I think it's on her knee, ask your mother."

"Is she going to die?"

"Probably, if we're lucky."

"Whose room is she sleeping him? She is not sleeping in my room I have just had it decorated in red and black and all my posters and everything..."

"She stayed in my room last time it's your turn."

"I don't care you're a dweeb so that doesn't count."

"At least I don't worship Dracula and wear stupid looking shoes."

"Children, children, for goodness sake stop squabbling," David felt the need to pull rank, "She is not sleeping in anybody's room, she is going to stay downstairs on the sofa bed until her knee gets better, or at least until she has her leg amputated."

Both of the children's faces lit up at the thought of this fact. "Is she going to have her leg amputated, dad?" Simon squealed with delight.

"No she is not and for goodness sake don't go telling your mother that I said she was, otherwise we will all be in trouble. Your mother is worried enough as it is." Truthfully it was only David that was worried, but he could do without Jessica berating him for telling the kids that granny was about to have her leg amputated, adding to his woes. Over and over he kept telling himself that it would only be for a short while and then it would all be over. David's only glimmer of hope now being that he had managed to convince his beloved wife

16

to let him replace the battered and worn out goggle box with a brand new television. He clung to this notion like a drowning man clinging to a wooden chest, bobbing about in the harsh sea, with no land in sight.

The children disappeared upstairs. Jessica was next door chatting to the neighbours about their daughter's wedding plans. David fraught with anxiety decided to call his old school mate and best friend Mark. After a messy divorce Mark, who was assured by his deranged ex-wife that he would never see the girls again, moved down to Cornwall with a young woman thirteen years his junior, that he had met on a camping holiday in France. At first David was outraged and a little bit astonished and even slightly jealous, but that was a long time ago and Mark had a new family now what with the birth of his son Zak.

The phone rang for ages, it always rang for ages with Mark, sometimes he answered, sometimes he just let it ring.

"Hello."

"Hi Mark it's me David."

"Davey boy, how's it hanging?" If anybody else had dared to call him 'Davey boy' he would have killed them there and then on the spot, somehow from Mark it felt like a compliment.

"Well you know..." plainly Mark did not know, "same old shit, different day." They both laughed as though that old joke was still funny.

"How's Jess?"

"She's fine."

"And the kids are they being good?"

"Yeah."

" How old is your oldest now, what is she called again...Leila?" Mark was Lucy's Godparent, he could at least try to remember her name.

"Lucy."

"Lucy that's it, she must be, what, twelve, thirteen?"

"Fifteen, next month."

"My God time flies. What's up, buddy"

No messing about with Mark, direct and to the point, he knew David well enough to know that he would never have called him on a Thursday evening unless he was concerned about something.

"Jessica's mother is coming to stay."

"The Dragon Queen...but you hate her."

"Yeah, apparently she is having her knee operated on and she has to stay here to recuperate."

"Maybe you should kill her." David hoped he was joking.

"Thought about it but you know what with the law and everything..." they both laughed.

"Well I say baton down the hatches, grin and bear it and as soon as it is all over come down to Cornwall and we will all go out and celebrate. We would love to see you. Zak is walking now, you should see him he gets everywhere." Going down to Cornwall was Marks answer to everything and who knows he was probably right, after all it worked for Mark. Maybe there was something invigorating in that salty sea air.

"Do you know I might just do that, I will have to ask Jessica, of course." Like almost every couple in the country David was not averse to blaming his partner if he wanted to get out of something.

"Well good luck and I will speak to you soon, yeah."

"Yeah, take care now," and with that Mark was gone.

After he had hung up the silence hovered around the room like a heavy fog. There was the dull boom, boom, boom of whatever kind of grunge music Lucy was into this week, and some kind of weird thudding sound coming out of Simon's room, but for David the silence was downright ethereal. Not ready to settle down for a nights entertainment on the television he opted to get a beer from the fridge. This is my world, my demesne, thought David as he glanced around the living room, sometimes he forgot that there were three other people living in the house, it may not be much but it is mine. Jessica's mum had not even arrived yet and he still felt judged. David was on the verge of becoming positively maudlin when he heard the tell tale signs of Jessica coming in through the back door. Thank God, he thought!

18

"You never guess what Harry and Jane have gone and hired for the wedding," Jessica shouted into the living room.

David did not care but he welcomed the distraction, "Dunno," he called back.

"Only a replica carriage of the one that Katie Price had when she married Peter Andre," said Jessica walking into the living room. "You know the one, it's all pink and white and looks like something Cinderella would use."

David thought it sounded like a dystopian nightmare, "That's nice," he replied.

"And they are all going to eat poisoned sugar-mice during the service." Jessica continued, a look of consternation crossing her face, a look that David failed to spot.

"Great."

"Now I know something is wrong, David. Spit it out...what is it?"

"Nothing, nothing at all, everything is fine."

Jessica knew him too well. "You're worried about mother coming next week aren't you?"

"No not at all," he lied unconvincingly.

"Look darling," her voice softened and she came right over to sit beside him, "I promise it will only be for a few days and I will do my level best to keep her out of your way. If it gets really bad you can always hide out in Harry's shed like you do when I am cleaning out the kitchen cupboards," and then she added laughing, "Don't think I don't know what you boys get up to in there."

David fell in love with her all over again, right at that moment, and he remembered why he married her, "I don't know what you mean," he replied with a silly grin on his face.

Later that night they made love and to David it felt like Blackpool all over again, but that was another story.

Chapter Five

So here they were Saturday morning, one week before the event horizon, doing the weekly shop in the local superstore. David stared around at the faces of the dead, zombies looking for the cheapest deal on soap powder and the like, and he questioned his humanity. David's role in this necessary evil was to push the trolley back and forth up and down the aisles and to look helpless. Occasionally he would grab the odd packet of biscuits, or bar of chocolate, and try to avoid Jessica's disapproving looks as they continued their journey through the underworld.

Today was different, today once they had finished buying their goods they were going back into the store to get a new television. David could barely contain his excitement. "Stop it," Jessica turned to him, smiling, "You're acting like a big kid."

"What are you on about?" he replied. David knew exactly what she was on about.

"The way you are spinning that trolley, you are going to injure someone in a minute, now just stop!"

Suitably reprimanded David carried on his way with only the odd sideways push of the trolley as an act of defiance.

The checkouts were crammed solid. It did not matter which one they chose, they knew it would always be the one that took the longest. They queued meekly. Hell froze over. At last there was only one person in front of them. This was Jessica's world she began unloading the goods onto the belt, frozen stuff at the front, then the tins, then the toiletries, then packet stuff and so on, and so on until they finally hit the bread which always had to be last. David could barely watch, left to his own devices he would just bung the stuff into the bags willy-nilly, after all it only had to survive the twenty minutes or so of the journey home. David was not known for his organisational skills. On the odd occasion when he had to pick up some goods on his own, under strict instructions from Jessica on what to get, he just got flustered under the intense glare of the checkout operator and panicked, stuffing everything in together crushing bread and spilling washing up liquid over everything. At these times he knew he was in for a rollicking when he got home but by then it was too late, the deed had been done, faux pas committed.

The woman in front of them had decided to give the bored looking teenage cashier her entire life history. Just put the damn shopping into the bags, thought David, and then we can all get on with our lives. "...what with the car playing up and everything, I tell you it has been one of those weeks," continued the grizzled harridan, oblivious to the rest of the human race. At last after what seemed like an eternity she finally decided to pay, but then she could not find her store card and she was sure that she had a voucher in the bottom of her purse. David wished her dead, mostly he only considered capital punishment for murderers and child sex offenders but today he was prepared to make an exception. Even Jessica was frowning and in David's world that meant things were really serious.

Free of the shopping, which had been safely stored away in the back of the car, they returned into the store victorious. David headed straight for a bank of television screens all showing the same advertisement. Jessica wandered off.

"Can I help you," said a rather pleasant looking young man in store uniform.

"As a matter of fact you can." David was feeling positively smug, "we want to buy a new television."

"Very good sir, I notice you looking at this one." Nobody on the planet could fail to miss the one he was looking at it was the biggest one in the store.

"Yeah, how much is that one?" Like all grown up boys David wanted the biggest toys.

"Well first of all let me tell you a little bit about it." Ominously David noted that he diverted the price question. "It is already internet enabled so you can straight away link it in with your computer and other wi-fi, it goes without saying that you have the capability for 3D vision if you buy the compatible equipment, and then there is digital picture within picture facility which means you can watch one

21

programme while keeping an eye on up to two other stations. This particular model has advanced dio-chromatic technology which means that the picture will always look crystal clear wherever you sit in the room from any angle. It also has a satellite linked guide which allows you to watch any programme you might have missed within the last fourteen days and is programmable up to three months in advance..." David now realised that although this young man was disguised as an affable store assistant, he was in fact a quantum physicist taking time out from redesigning the Hadron Collider to sell televisions. The professor continued, "Then we come to the sound quality where you have thirty-two settings which allow for everything from action movies, to stadium arenas, but to experience the best sound you might want to set it up in 7.1 mode where you will get the full cinema experience, although that would require extra speakers."

What the Hell are you talking about, thought David, while actually saying, "That sounds great." Why had he not brought Simon with him, as far as David was concerned the fellow was talking in Mandarin, Simon could have translated. He pressed on, "Did you say how much it cost, I can't remember?" David remembered.

"This particular model is on a Managers special this week and could be yours for just under two thousand."

David reeled. Did he just say two grand? You could get a second hand car for that kind of money. "Do you have any models that just have television programmes?" he asked, sounding like a small town hick from the country, and feeling like one too.

The smartly dressed young man looked positively insulted, "Well we do have the Base-rate model which is only 42 inches, and has none of the features, but you do get a three year warranty."

"That's the one," the country bumpkin continued, "What sort of price is that one?"

"We retail that one at just over three hundred pounds"

Nirvana. "We'll take it." David declared, and the matter was settled.

Jessica appeared from nowhere just as he was about to pay. Where had she been? How did she know that the transaction was almost done? "For an extra twenty-five pounds we can have it delivered, would you like it delivered? It can take from four to five days."

Four to five days, David could hardly wait four to five minutes, "No thank you," he courteously replied, "we can put it in the back of the car."

"Very well, sir. There is just the matter of the form for the television licence authority, and some warranty documentation, and we are there."

David signed his life away. He did not care, all he wanted was the television back at home and ready to watch. Finally the deed was done and he waved goodbye to the affable nuclear scientist as they pushed the television, half in and half out of the trolley, out of the store and into the car park.

Back at the car David struggled to get the television inside amid the rest of the shopping. "You should have had it delivered," Jessica crowed.

"I was trying to save you money," David retaliated. Finally after much manoeuvring, and possibly a few broken eggs, he got the box inside and they were on their way.

At last they were home, Jessica retreated to the kitchen where she hoped to reassemble the carnage that had once been the weekly shop, and David was left in the front room staring at the monolith waiting to be removed from its box. There was nothing he could do about it he would have to venture into the no man's land of the kitchen to get a knife so he could attack the packaging, he hoped Jessica would not stab him with it.

Ten minutes later, and a living room that was covered in polystyrene and cardboard, he had released the television from its incarceration. Now came the tricky bit, disconnecting the old model from the massive amount of wires that gave it life support, and reconnecting the new one that was to replace it. David did his level best and after an impressive bout of heaving and shoving that surely would have impressed the strongest weightlifter, he had the old television on the floor and the new boy firmly in place. It took another twenty minutes and several failures but eventually he felt

23

that every lead was in the corresponding socket and this baby was ready to go. Triumphant it plugged his new toy in and....nothing!! Nothing at all!! There had to be an on/off switch, frantically he hit all of the grey buttons on the side of the casing, still nothing. There must be another button he had missed, maybe underneath the screen, maybe at the back, he inspected every discernible inch of the television in vain. After a while it dawned on him that maybe it worked off the remote control. At last he found the remote along with a manual, warranty documents and some other paraphernalia hidden in the bottom of the cardboard box. He put the specially provided batteries into the controller and pressed what looked like an on/off button, on the grounds that it seemed different from the dozens of other buttons, and had the word 'standby' written under it. Still nothing, for Christ's sake what more do you want I have given you everything. Deflated David sat down and decided to read the manual.

Time passed, he waded through several languages, and then pages of waffle, and at last the index guided him to page thirty-two, 'Operating Instructions.' He read on, 'Using the remote device press and hold for five seconds the red button marked 'standby' and point towards the screen.' So he had been right all along, David felt partially absolved. He followed the instructions and after a few seconds a tiny green light appeared under the screen. David almost ejaculated.

Jessica heard his screams of delighted. "Is it working?" she asked, poking her head around the living room door. The screen remained dark.

"No, but I've got a green light." He could barely keep it in, he felt like he was going to burst. Jessica pulled a face and decided to admonish him about the state of the front room instead. Under the circumstances David decided to help her clear away the mess and cart the old television upstairs to the bedroom, after all a man could not have too much excitement for one day.

"Where is Simon?" he asked Jessica. Simon never went anywhere, today when you need him he had vanished.

"You know, I told you, he has gone into town to get his book signed by that bloke who wrote about time travel or something," she answered.

"Bloody typical, today of all days. Do you think Lucy knows anything about televisions?"

"Lucy's not here either she has gone to see her friend in Edmunton."

David decided that there was only one thing for it he would have to read the manual and try to get the damn thing working. He settled down with a cup of tea and some digestives. It seemed that his new television could perform miracles according to the instruction booklet. It could even tap into the Pentagon defence computer and defend itself from nuclear attack, or at least in David's mind, but the only thing it could not do was turn itself on. 'Set Up – Initialising The TT120N. - Before you can begin to enjoy the TT120N you must first tune in the digital programme receptor to the frequencies in your area. 1) Go into the Menu screen and using the up and down buttons on the remote select the 'Automatic Tune' icon.' Only two people in David's universe knew what the Hell any of this gibberish meant, one worked in a local superstore selling electrical goods, and the other was getting his book signed. He read the words over and over again hoping that they would suddenly become intelligible, they did not, in fact, they became even more indistinguishable. He tried singing the words in his head to the Disney classic 'Bare Necessities', they still made no sense. He even considered prayer.

"I might drive into town and see if I can spot Simon anywhere," he announced to Jessica.

"No you are not, leave him alone, it is not his fault you can't get the thing working. Let me have a look"

Reluctantly and a little sheepishly David handed over the manual for her perusal. She stared at it for a bit while David slurped his tea. "Did you hold the standby button down for five seconds?" she asked.

"I've done that." David snapped back. "God at times you can be so stupid."

"And you pressed the blue menu button." David's world fell apart. Jessica pressed the blue button on the remote and from nowhere a drop-down menu appeared on the screen. He hated her but at the same time felt elated that they were getting somewhere.

"Give it here," David snatched the remote out of her hands, acting like a petulant child.

"I was only trying to help," Jessica retorted.

David selected 'Automatic Tune' and a bar appeared at the bottom of the screen slowly the bar turned blue, it looked like it was doing something. The expectant father looked on, there was a moment of tension as the screen once more went completely dark and then 'Bingo' there it was real television. No sex was ever this good, well maybe, but not for today. David could hear Angels trumpeting from the heavens. From nowhere the infamous words of the poet Shelley rang in his ears, 'My name is Ozymandias, king of kings: Look on my works, ye Mighty, and despair!' Just for a moment David ruled everything and the universe was his to command. If he could beat this electrical device he could do anything, anything at all. Jessica brought him back down to Earth, "Try Channel Three I think that my dancing programme is about to start." Is that it? David had mastered the universe and all she could say is, "Can we watch Channel Three?"

With a shrug of his shoulders David flipped the television over to Channel Three. So while Jessica sat back and watched the ballroom dancers waltzing their way around the studio, David sat back and admired the pretty colours. Marital bliss.

Chapter Six

The following Monday David returned to work. "Did you get up to much over the weekend?" asked Eric, chewing the cud.

"As a matter of fact I did," David hung is colours to the mast, "I bought a new television, the picture on it is amazing!'

"Oh yeah, did you have much trouble tuning it in?"

"Nah, it was so easy even a child could do it." A child did. A very big child.

Felicity, who had gone to get some more staples for her stapling gun, returned to the office breathless. "Have you heard the news?" she asked the room in general. It was a rhetorical question, none of them were psychic. They stared at her gormlessly and shook their heads. "Rachel from accounting has committed suicide." This was almost information overload the room went deathly silent as they each tried to digest this in their own way.

"What happened?" asked Adam inquisitively.

"Nobody knows but apparently she had a row with her boyfriend and he dumped her."

"Which one is Rachel?" David felt the need to enquire.

"You know, the young one with ginger hair."

"Oh her," David barely knew the girl.

"I would have shagged her," chimed Eric, never one to shy away from saying the worst thing possible.

"Could you at least pretend to show a little respect, Eric," Andrew interjected, trying to bring some decorum to the proceedings.

"But it is true, I would have shagged her, she didn't have to kill herself." If this was a defence surely it was the most lamentable ever.

"How did she die? How did they know she was dead?" Adam continued his Spanish inquisition.

"Well apparently Rachel's mum phoned the office this morning to let them know what is going on and the police were involved and everything. Marion was crying her eyes out she is devastated."

Marion was head honcho in the accounts department, and was the one person everybody went to if they had a problem with their wages, because she was the only one capable of putting it right.

"I remember there was a lad back at school who killed himself," Ronald looked up from his desk, "Some say that it was because his team lost their football match, but most people thought it was because Mr Eddy the games master touched him up. They were a different kind of sex offender in those days none of your paedophile lot." What the Hell did Ronnie mean by that, David wondered, were they a better type of offender back then, was he implying that it was better, or perhaps even worse, to be molested back in the good old days. God knows, David decided that the best option was not to clutter his mind with such matters.

Felicity acted like she had not heard Ronald, "I am not sure what happened but from the gist of the conversation Marion had with the Rachel's mum I think the girl took an overdose."

"Truly an awful thing, such a waste of human life," David felt compelled to say. And with that the matter was concluded all of the information had been disseminated. The meat gleaned from the bones. Everybody went back to their work. The morning coffee would have a bitter aftertaste today.

Distracted from his work by this Shakespearian tragedy David looked around at his fellow office workers, his compadres, and began to ponder how little he really knew about them. Sure they chatted over lunch breaks and exchanged pleasantries, and there was the odd Christmas party which usually ended up as a fiasco, but when they went home at night, and at the weekends they had their own private lives, their own little worlds. What were their families like? Did they live in posh furnished houses or shabby run down flats in squalor, or perhaps they still lived at home with mum and dad as in Adams case? Did they worry about money problems, or an elderly relative, or the state of the world? What were their views on politics, religion, wars, famine, drugs? He decided to break down some of these barriers. "Eric, have you ever thought about starting a family?" he asked, with polite curiosity.

"Why who have you been talking to?" This was not the response he expected. "Has that bitch said something?" This was positively hostile David began to regret ever asking the question.

He turned to Adam, hoping to diffuse the situation, "What about you Adam would you ever want to have kids?" David was painfully aware that Eric's gaze was searing into the back of his neck.

"I don't want kids, they ruin everything. I'd sooner spend my money on a new car," said Adam.

"What do you think, Felicity?" and then he remembered. Oh Christ! Why did I not just keep my bloody big mouth shut? Felicity just stared at David straight in the face, a sort of silent angry look. David floundered, he hoped he might faint, desperately he looked around, there was Ronald in the corner, but Ronald's wife had left him taking the children with her when the money disappeared.

"Mrs Smith and I thought about having more children," Andrew arrived in the ambulance. It never ceased to amaze David where your rescuer came from in these darkest hours. David was so relieved he almost forgot to question what sort of a man calls their wife by their surname. "After Damien was born we decided to try for a sister, or a brother, but she had a problem with her fallopian tubes so we gave up on the idea."

David decided not to delve any deeper into the matter, whatever problem Mrs Smith had with her internal tubing would be buried in the archives, forgotten about and never mentioned again. David remonstrated himself for ever wanting to get to know these people in the first place, after all, life's circumstances had brought them together not friendship. The only vested interest they had in each other's lives was to keep the lifeboat afloat, so they could all get paid by the Harman and Cooke Insurance Agency once a month.

The tension in the office was positively palpable and not because there had been a death in the family. Eric was tapping his pen and staring at his computer screen with a furrowed look that would have worried Jehova, Ronald was gazing out of the window lost in his own reverie and Adam was looking perplexed. What on earth was he perplexed about? David dared to glance over in Felicity's direction. Were those tears in her eyes? This was really too much, twice in one lifetime, Andrew was going to have to say something. Andrew seemed to be the only person in the workplace completely oblivious to the blackening atmosphere. "David, do you have the stats on the Third Party Fire and Theft settlement claims? Could you e-mail them to me, please."

"I will do it right now." David was happy for the distraction. If I ever manage to survive this day, he thought, I will never open my big mouth again.

Later that day as the dust settled and the work place became the usual breeding ground for tedium and monotony, David reflected on recent events. Work and home life are two separate entities and never the twain shall meet, he cogitated, internally he vowed to protect his family from these Machiavellian forces of evil, he would be their unseen knight protector, it was for the greater good, a matter of honour, he must be their unsung hero.

Five o'clock came on this painfully slow day from Hell, and with much relief everybody started to get ready to go home. Adam was always first out the door, he was like a tethered greyhound waiting to be released from its trap, the moment the second hand reached the twelve he was gone. Silently the others gathered their stuff and one by one shuffled towards the exit. "David can I have a quick word," Andrew called out. Oh my God is he really asking me to stay behind like a naughty schoolboy, thought David. The naughty child did as he was told.

"As you know, David, one day I am hoping to become regional manager for this area, and as my potential successor I really must have a word with you about getting along with other members of staff."

Incredulous, David gaped, he really was getting a lecture on morality from Dr Faustus.

David could not think of anything to say, the absurdity of the situation froze his mind. "Yes, Andrew."

"Some of them are a little bit 'sensitive' about certain issues," Andrew continued, "So a small degree of diplomacy would be the wisest choice, OK."

"OK, Andrew," David croaked. Andrew gave him a wan smile and made things worse by giving him a paternal pat on the back. David felt nauseated beyond belief, he was surely going to be sick here and now on the spot. It all came flooding back to him every reason why he disliked this loathsome reptile he called his boss, forgetting that only a short while ago he had hailed him as his rescuer, his saviour. He staggered out the door any semblance of normality having left his life a long time ago.

Chapter Seven

David pulled the car into the driveway and revelled in the security and the sanctity of the place he called 'home'. He went straight into the kitchen where Jessica was peeling some potatoes for their supper, "You would never guess what happened at work today," he said.

Jessica looked up from her task, "Enlighten me."

Was that a hint of sarcasm in her voice, never-the-less David was too caught up in his own excitement to let it stop him now, "Well first of all Rachel, the young girl in accountants, committed suicide and then..."

"What at work?" Jessica interrupted.

"No not at work over the weekend... something to do with her boyfriend leaving her and then..."

"How did she die?" Jessica interrupted again.

"Why does everybody want to know how she died? What does it matter? I think that it was an overdose or something. Stop interrupting me."

"But I am trying to establish the facts," said Detective Inspector Jessica neglecting her duties as a wife and mother and turning into Scotland Yard's finest.

"Anyway I got to asking Eric about his thoughts on children and he got angry, and then the whole office turned against me and, even worse, Andrew made me stay behind and gave me a talking to, it was awful."

Inspector Jessica was going to need all of her interrogational skills if she were to disassemble David's previous statement and make any sense of it at all. "Start at the beginning why did you ask Eric his thoughts on children?"

"I just trying to be friendly, I guess."

"So why did that make him angry?"

"Well I suspect that Lolita probably wants kids, or maybe they are infertile or something, who knows?"

"So what made the rest of them angry?"

"You tell me. I think children are a really sore subject in our office."

"And Andrew said that to you did he?"

"No he just told me that I ought to work on my people skills, and then he patted me on the back. Good God, I may even have to change jobs."

"Stop being a drama queen, I am sure it is not as bad as you are making it out to be," and with that D.I. Jessica returned to her vegetables.

David was stumped. "What's for tea?" he asked, a change of subject being the best tactic here.

"Sausage and mash." There was at least was something to be enjoyed about this day, thought David.

"Oh by the way Lucy has got her friend here, so make sure you are on your best behaviour."

"I am always on my best behaviour," pleaded the plaintiff, who was fortunate enough not to see the face that his wife had pulled.

On cue Lucy appeared at the kitchen door, half obscured David could see a figure behind her. "Hi Dad, this is my friend Jack."

It felt like a bomb exploding by the kitchen sink. Did somebody just hit me in the face with a cricket bat? David tried to speak, the words would not come out. "Uuhh.."

"Does Jack want a glass of juice or anything?" he heard Jessica say somewhere under the water.

"No thank you Mrs Banks, I'm fine." It speaks.

"Well be sure to let us know if you do, also I there are some iced buns in the tin if you are feeling hungry."

"Thanks mum, you're the best," said Lucy reaching for the tin.

David stared in horror as Lucy grabbed two of the buns, she passed one to the intruder and kept one for herself and then with a wave of their hands and a quick smile they were gone. At first he could not move or speak, reality was a thing of the past, everything went hazy, it was like reliving his conversation with Andrew all over again, all of a sudden he was back in the room. "Who the fuck is that?" he hissed at Jessica. David only used the f-word when things had gone from bad to worse.

"I told you, last week, Lucy was having her friend over for the evening."

"That is not a friend, Jessica Langley," he only used her maiden name when she was in real trouble, "that is a boy."

"What does it matter? Boy, girl, he is helping Lucy with her homework, I thought you'd be pleased."

"Friends," he continued, oblivious to her response, "help you to decide what dress to wear to the local dance. Friends show you how to put on mascara without smudging your face. Friends sit down and watch romantic videos and pass each other tissues when the hero dies," David's voice was getting louder, "that is not a friend that is a boy. Boys pull the legs off spiders, they play football and they have only one thing on their minds and I think we both know what that is."

"Don't be so bloody daft," they were both swearing now, Jessica was raising her voice too, "this is the twenty-first century not the 1950's things have changed, David Banks." Full name as well, this argument was scaling new heights.

"Just when I thought this day could not get any worse you have managed to surpass my deepest nightmares. Well done!!"

"Now you are just being stupid. Maybe it is good for Lucy to have friends. You are always saying that you wished Simon would get out more and make some new friends."

"She is fifteen years old for Christ's sake. Oh my God, they could be having sex right now and in my house." David had to fight the urge to run upstairs and drag the boy out by his hair.

"Don't you trust your daughter." Jessica almost screamed. David trusted his daughter, it was the one saving grace.

"I do, I really do..." David felt helpless. Momentarily he wanted to cry. And then it all came flooding back to him the reason why the girl in accounting had killed herself. He wanted to explain this to his wife in the most reasonable voice he could muster, which under the circumstances was quite difficult, "Jessica that is not a boy, that is a murderer."

34

"What the Hell are you on about."

"He is a murderer, don't you get it that is why the girl in work killed herself."

"Now you are being just plainly idiotic."

"But don't you see," the inplausibility of his argument eluded him, "he is going to break her heart, and you caused it all. I hope you are ready to pick up the pieces because I'm certainly not going to." Suddenly it was all Jessica's fault.

They ate tea in silence, the bangers and mash normally so tasty might has well been made of cardboard. Even the new television conspired against him showing only programmes where young boys dated girls. I must have gone to bed last night and woke up in purgatory, David speculated, or worse still, maybe this is Groundhog Day and I am doomed to live it over and over again. "How is he getting home?" David chose to break the silence. He hoped that he was not supposed to give the boy a lift home that would be adding insult to injury, there was no way under the sun that this lad was staying the night.

"One of his parents are picking him up at nine," Jessica responded.

"And they know how to find the house?" he enquired.

"Yeah, the kids were dropped off after school."

"Ok."

The evening went slow, too slow, but finally the appointed hour arrived and David heard a car pull up in the driveway. Unable to resist he peered through the curtains. "Whoever it is they have got a nice car," he said to Jessica, "it looks new. There is a man getting out, he seems quite normal." David watched as the man approached the door and then dived back to his seat as though he had not moved all evening. The doorbell rang, Jessica went out into the hall to answer it.

"Hello, my name is Michael," said the stranger, in a friendly manner, "I've come to pick up my son, Jack."

"Nice to meet you," said Jessica, "my name is Jessica and this is my husband David." She pointed towards David, through the open living room door. David was busy pretending to read a magazine he had just picked up.

"Hello there," said David, looking up from the journal.

Jessica shouted up the stairs, "Lucy, Jack's dad is here."

"Ok, mum." was the muffled reply.

As they waited Jack's dad looked around nervously and as David peered at him he suddenly became aware, just for a moment, of something in the man's eyes. It was probably nothing but it felt like...like...looking in a mirror. In a blinding flash of light David had a 'Eureka' moment. This man was just like him, he could sense it, this man worried about his son wanting a tattoo, or having parts of his body pierced, or hanging out with potential junkies, or carrying knives. This man was a father. David jumped up, "I don't think I introduced myself properly," he said, reaching out to shake his hand. "David Banks."

"Michael Ripley," the man responded, shaking David's hand, a look of relief crossing his face.

"Come in, come in, you don't have to stand there in the doorway," said David, "It must be freezing out there."

Dutifully the man entered, looking slightly more relaxed, he turned to David and said, "I was a bit worried about what you would think about my son being friends with your daughter. I didn't know if that might make you feel uncomfortable, he is a good lad and everything but you know some parents might not like it."

David loved this man, David wanted to kiss this man, my God perhaps they should dump their wives and try to raise the children properly. "Don't be so stupid this is the modern world, we are not living in the past now." David laughed, deliberately averting his wife's eyes.

The man smiled back, "Phew that is a relief, it was just..." and at that moment both teenagers came bounding down the stairs. "Don't forget to thank Mr and Mrs Banks for having you," said the new paragon of virtue.

"Thank you for having me over," said the boy, and then turned to Lucy saying, "Catch you in school later, yeah?"

"Yeah," said Lucy.

Mum, dad and daughter watched as the car pulled out of the drive and then they were gone. At this point David was ahead of the game and probably should have gone back to his television and spent the rest of the evening in harmonious peace, but a small kernel of nagging doubt had wormed its way into his brain and it grew and grew. He knew it was wrong, and he knew that he should not say it, but the words sort of formed in his mouth and even though he tried to stop them they sort of flowed out of his lips, so he turned to Lucy and asked, "You're not pregnant are you?"

"Dad!" Lucy half shouted, half whined and instantly spun around and stormed off up the stairs.

Jessica looked angry. Jessica looked very angry. "You have to ruin everything, don't you?"

David did not even try to deny it, it was probably true.

Chapter Eight

The next few days went surprisingly well for David Banks. The mood in the office had positively lightened. Every so often he would glance over at Andrew and be slightly unnerved to see his boss smiling at him, in a sickeningly patronising way, but other than that things went well. In fact, they were all in such good cheer that by Thursday morning Adam had been dispatched to get some cream cakes under strict instructions not to get anything that involved cinnamon.

Eric seemed to have forgotten their spat and at one point bought David a cup of coffee from the vending machine which was his way of saying 'sorry'. David, in turn, lent Eric his pen knowing that he would never see it again, which was his way of reciprocating the gesture. They were friends again, that was all that was important. Even Felicity seemed in a good mood. How quickly she had gotten over the death of her feline companion. Maybe females are made of sterner stuff than men, David surmised. Ronald and Adam, well they were just Ronald and Adam.

They talked about the weather, game shows on television, the ever increasing price of food, the cost of petrol, the best place to get a decent Bolognese, all manner of subjects. They never ever talked about politics or children, especially children. And then, of course....

"Do you think England can win the football this year?" Adam asked Eric, but in reality the whole room. Everyone agreed that this was the year that they could do it, even Felicity and she hated football. Things really were on the up.

Back at home things were improving, also, Jessica had finished cleaning the entire house and had repositioned the furniture so that her mother would be as comfortable as possible. Much to Simon's dismay they had stolen his single bed and left him with a camp bed mattress so that 'granny' could sleep downstairs in relative ease. Unusually for the pair, they had ventured into supermarket zombieland and done the weekly shop mid-week to get it out of the way early. Things really were coming together for the royal visit.

The plan was for Jessica to take her car over to her mum's place on Friday afternoon, so that she could go with her mother to the hospital and help take care of her, before and after the operation, and then to bring her mum back to their place on Saturday, all being well. David liked this plan. David liked this plan a lot. It meant that he could enjoy one last night of freedom before the dragon arrived, and he had Jessica's permission to buy pizza for him and the kids. David decided not to tell Jessica about the copious amounts of alcohol he intended for dessert, some things are best left unsaid, besides, he figured Jessica already knew of his intentions but chose prudently to remain silent on the issue. Every condemned man is entitled to a last meal.

The only fly in the ointment of what was turning into a perfect week, was an unusual letter sent home from school requesting Jessica and David book an appointment with the headmaster about their son Simon. David read the letter three times after Jessica had showed it to him. "Are you sure it says Simon and not Lucy?" he asked, even though the evidence was there in black and white in front of him, "Maybe they made a mistake and got the wrong name."

Normally it might have irked Jessica that David was being hard on Lucy, but having had letters sent home twice before about their daughter's behaviour she let it ride. "It may be nothing," said Jessica, "perhaps they are just giving us a progress report."

"What sort of progress report."

"I don't know, I was just saying for example."

"Do you think he is being bullied?"

"If he is, he never said."

"They don't like the brainy ones, the other children, we used to torment them in our school, don't you remember that fat kid, Joe something or other."

"That was thirty years ago I am pretty sure things have moved on since our day."

"But what can it be?"

39

"I told you I don't know. We will just have to wait until next week and then we can find out."

David decided he could not wait until next week. "I might have a quick word with him, you know, man to man stuff, see if he is being bullied."

"Don't you dare," said Jessica, "you will only make things worse, you know you will."

David ignored her and bounded up the stairs before Jessica could stop him. He gently knocked on Simon's bedroom door. "Come in," called a voice from the interior.

David opened the door and there sat Simon cross legged on the new mattress, games controller in one hand, a far-away look on his face, he seemed almost eerie in the luminous glow of the monitor screen. "I just wanted to make sure you were comfortable with the new mattress, son," said David.

"Yeah, it's a bit 'trick' but you get used to it." That word again.

"Other than that is everything alright," David tried to sound casual, "no problems at school or anything?"

"Only that they had to cancel the physics lesson. Mr Baxter had to go early because his wife is having a baby," The boy seemed genuinely disappointed, most boys his age would have jumped for joy if the physics lesson had been cancelled.

David sat down on the bed next to his son, not an easy manoeuvre as the camp bed mattress was a darn sight lower than he had thought. "Do you have many friends in school, Simon?" David asked, still trying to keep it casual.

"Well there is Martin, he can be a bit 'trick'," David was starting to hate that word, "but most of the time he's ok."

"And the other boys, do you get on with them alright?"

"Not bad they do their thing, I do mine."

"You would tell me or your mother if they were giving you a hard time, wouldn't you son."

"Yeah."

"And you do know that you could talk to us about anything if you were in any sort of trouble, anything at all, don't you Simon?"

"I'm not in any trouble, dad," Simon responded, and then with a quizzical look on his face added, "am I?"

"No, no," answered David, "I was just making sure you were ok." And with a paternal smile, because they had outgrown the kiss on the cheek, David got up and left the room.

Back down the stairs Jessica was waiting, "Well...?" she asked.

"He doesn't know anything."

"I hope you haven't gone and upset him."

"No I have not," David pleaded not guilty, "I just asked him if everything was alright in school."

"Did you tell him about the letter?" Jessica asked sternly.

"No I didn't, what do you take me for," David thanked God that he forgot to mention the letter.

Stumped by this impossible enigma they both sat down to watch the new television. After an extensive channel flip because David had the remote control, they eventually settled down to watch some awful drama about a love affair between a disabled actress and a former racing driver. Neither of them really liked the programme but nor could either of them suggest a viable alternative. In due time the play ended, much to David's relief, and if truth be told Jessica's, also. This was followed by a brief summary of the news and then the announcer declared, "There now follows a documentary which some viewers might find distressing." Sounds promising already, thought David. "It contains a harrowing report of the high suicide rate in unusually gifted children." David and Jessica stared at each other in mute silence, they both looked like they had seen a ghost.

"Let's get an early night," suggested David.

"Good idea," said Jessica. They turned the television off.

Later that night, despite this horrific turn of events, they did not feel traumatised enough not to enjoy sex in the usual way. After all, Jessica was off to get mum in the morning why waste a golden opportunity, this could be their last chance for quite some time.

Chapter Nine

The following morning breakfast was a chaotic event. Apart from David getting ready for work and the children getting ready for school they had the additional factor of Jessica getting ready to go to her mums. The kids had been suitably primed as to be on their best behaviour when granny was here, a feat that David saw as nigh on impossible, and David had also been prepped by Jessica to at least try to get along with her mother if only to keep the peace. Miracles have happened, thought David. For his part, David had agreed to leave work early and pick the children up from school and, with one final admonishment from Jessica about making sure the house was tidy for when she got back, they went their separate ways.

The gossip at work was that Adam might have got himself a new girlfriend. Nothing unusual there but this one did seem more promising as she had agreed to go on a 'date' with him to the cinema.

"What's she like?" asked Felicity.

"Pretty, she is always laughing," Adam replied.

"Where did you meet her?" Felicity continued her line of investigation.

"Well actually it was through her friend on Facebook." Although this was not truly an explanation of how they met, considering the mysterious world of the online site to non-members it had to suffice.

What does she do for a living?" Felicity went on.

"She is training to be a nail beautician."

"Oh," said Felicity.

"More to the point does she have big tits?" Eric chimed in. If 'big tits' were a necessary requirement for a successful relationship, then he and Lolita would have finished a long time ago.

"It's not just about the size of her knockers," Adam felt the need to defend himself, "There are more important things, you know."

"So that's a no then," said Eric, with a smug look on his face.

Everybody else felt the need to offer reassurance at this point, and to assure Adam that the most important thing was that he liked her, and she liked him.

"Whatever you do don't let her get hold of your cash," Ronald advised, "make sure she pays her half of everything. A bitter divorce, and old age, had not soured this man.

"Don't listen to any of them," said Felicity, the unspoken mother of the group, "Just you enjoy yourself and take it one day at a time."

As he drove away from the offices of Harman and Cooke Insurance Agency later that afternoon David intended to enjoy himself too. His first mission was to pick the children up from school, take them home to get changed, and then in a deviation to the plans outlined by his beloved wife, he intended to take them to the local burger joint where they could all indulge in the greasiest, unhealthiest, slap up calorie fest known to man, boy or girl.

"Where are we going?" he could hear the united voices of both children held captive in the back seat of the car.

"You will just have to wait and see."

"But mum said..." Lucy wailed.

"Never mind what mum said, we are going to have fun." David declared.

"Yeah," said Simon.

As they pulled up into the out of town burger restaurant car park, Lucy started to nag her father, "Mum doesn't like us eating here she says the food is really bad for us,"

"I know it's great, I am going to have double cheese-burger with cola and fries, and if you lot want you can have fluffy chocolate flake ice cream too."

The thought of such culinary delights silenced Lucy immediately. Simon's face lit up like a Christmas tree, "Bagsy the toy monkey," he laid claim.

"I don't want it anyway," said Lucy, and the matter was settled.

Inside the restaurant was very busy, it being a Friday, so David ushered the kids over to what seemed like the one remaining free table while he went off to place their order. Surprisingly both children were quite amenable about what they wanted to eat, somehow he expected arguments. David joined one of the three queues and waited. He watched patiently as the people in the other two queues received their orders and were replaced by more people waiting to be served, and then just as he thought he might die of old age he found himself at the front. Staring at him was a rather vacant looking teenager dressed in a yellow and red uniform, "Can I help you," said the young man.

"Yes please," said David, "I want three double cheeseburgers with fries, one cola, two chocolate flake fluffies, oh and no mayonnaise on the burgers, but can one of them have ketchup."

"Do you want fries with the cheeseburgers?"

David was confused, he thought that he had asked for fries, "..uumm yes, please."

"And you want mayonnaise."

"No...no mayonnaise but can I have ketchup on one of the burgers." David could not stop himself from looking at this young man and thinking, please do not live up to my preconceived stereotype. Perhaps this lad was a university student earning a bit of extra cash.

"What sort of cola do you want, regular or diet?"

Why would anyone, in their right mind, come into a restaurant that prides itself on giving any self respecting dietician nightmares and order diet cola, it made no sense. "Regular please," said David.

"So you want three cheeseburgers, one fries..."

"Let me stop you there," David interrupted, "I want three fries."

"Ok, and two burgers with mayonnaise one with ketchup..." David found himself resisting the urge to check whether this lad had put his underpants on outside of his trousers, could he even dress himself properly.

"No mayonnaise on any of the burgers, at any time," he was getting snappy now. "Write that down so you can remember."

"Regular cola, and fries, and two chocolate fluffies." The young man continued as though he had not heard David. "Do you want cola with the fluffies?"

"No thank you."

"What sort of cola?" They were communicating bit it felt like in two different languages.

"I think that we have already established that the one and only cola I am having is going to be regular." How hard could it be, the restaurant specialises in burgers it was not like they had to flambé freshly cooked scallops by the side of the table.

"That would be seventeen ninety-nine please," said the young man. David paid.

He joined his son and daughter at their table and they waited for the meal. Across from them some children were having what appeared to be a birthday party for about eight children. Judging from the size of them this was not an irregular occurrence. They struggled to be heard over the noise of these tiny birthday revellers. "Did you have a good day at school?" David asked Lucy.

"Pretty dull but it was ok."

"And your friend, what was he called, is he ok?"

"Jack, yeah he is ok, his parents are making him revise this weekend, he's got a maths test on Monday."

"What about you Simon, did you have a good day."

"We had a brilliant chemistry lesson where we looked at the effects of oxidisation on different metals. Did you know that some metals ignite when they are exposed to oxygen, dad?"

"No I didn't know that," answered David.

"Stop being a dweeb," said Lucy, "Dad doesn't care."

"I do care," said David. He did not really care.

"The only things you care about are make-up and stupid music." Simon accused Lucy.

"Come on kids, we are here to have fun not argue." This forced everybody into silence, so they sat and listened to the table next door singing 'Happy Birthday' to some enthralled child, as he was presented with a birthday cake by his mum. Time passed, David wondered what time the restaurant closed.

At last a young looking girl, dressed in the same uniform, came to their table carrying a tray of food and drinks, disguised with assorted packaging. "Did you order the cheeseburgers?" she asked anxiously.

"Yes that's us." David replied. She dropped the tray in front of them and was gone. On the tray were three colas, David wondered if they were diet or regular, one fries and three potential cheeseburgers. They also had two cartons of chocolate ice-cream drink and a small soft toy monkey. David looked around he could not see the inept young man and the other queues looked massive. "Fuck it, this will have to do," he said much to Lucy and Simon's amazement, mum really was away. He unwrapped his burger from the packaging, ravenous, and passed Lucy and Simon theirs. "You will just have to share the fries," he informed them. David took a bite, the first thing that he tasted was mayonnaise.

"Which one has got the ketchup?" asked Simon.

"Probably none of them," David replied, and he was right.

Chapter Ten

David woke up with the mother of all hangovers. How much did I drink last night, he wondered. It was the big day itself, the day of reckoning, and from the throbbing going on in the front of his brain it was not getting off to a good start. The smell of burnt toast wafting up the stairs was a strong giveaway that the children were already up. David tumbled out of bed and staggered off towards the shower. He revelled in the luxury of the hot water flowing over his skin and stepped out to face the world.

Downstairs was a bit of a mess but not beyond repair, the children were nowhere to be seen. The telephone rang he knew it would be Jessica even before he answered it. He had spoken to her last night in a bit of a drunken haze, he hoped that she had not noticed. "Hi, love, it's me Jessica."

"Hi darling."

"Have you sobered up yet?" She had noticed.

"I wasn't drunk," he lied.

"Anyway I was just calling to let you know that mum is out of the hospital and we are just leaving now. We will be there in about an hour."

"That's cool." Not necessarily cool but it was always going to be inevitable.

"You will give the place a tidy before we get there, won't you?" Less of a question, more of a command.

"It's already done," more lies, he had been lying a lot lately.

"Love you, bye."

"Love you too, bye."

After an hour, and some frantic tidying, David heard Jessica's car pull up in the drive. He stared out of the corner of the window and watched, as a hawk watches its prey, the only difference being that David was not sure if he was the prey. He watched Jessica's mother struggling to get out of the car, leg heavily bandaged, crutches everywhere and just for a moment he felt real compassion for the old girl, in fact, he even felt guilty for all of those feelings of animosity towards her. He heard the door open, "Come in mum," Jessica tried to assist her mother as best she could.

"Hello David," said her mother, with reasonable politeness.

"Hello Allison," said David, so that is how they were going to play it, let's pretend to be civil.

"Did you have a pleasant journey?" Even as he said it David realised that it sounded shallow, of course she did not have a pleasant journey she was in agony from the operation.

"Not too bad, the traffic was a bit heavy." Thank God she chose to ignore it.

"Would you like a cup of tea? David asked.

"That would be lovely, dear, you can put the kettle on as soon as you bring my things in from the car." And so it begins, thought David. "Now where's my lovely grandchildren."

The children were dutifully summoned from upstairs. Simon appeared first, "Hi Nan, how's it hanging?"

"My haven't you grown, your almost turning into a young man now, and so intelligent Jessica tells me, he gets that from his great uncle Rupert, you know." David had forgotten the unwritten rule, all positive traits and characteristics came from various members of Jessica's family and all of the negative traits, in her words, "...well, I don't know where he gets that from." The implication being that it was either directly from David or his ignoble brethren.

"You look so smart even out of school uniform," continued Simon's gran as she ruffled his hair, and then she reached inside her purse, which was no mean feat considering she had to balance the crutches at the same time, and produced a ten pound note which she crumpled up and stuffed into his shirt pocket.

Lucy came flying down the stairs, was it the smell of the money, "Hello nan," Lucy kissed her gran on the cheek, "Was the operation alright, not too painful, I hope?"

"Oh my angel, and so pretty too, it is so nice of you to ask, at least somebody cares," looking directly at David, even wounded she was still a dangerous animal. "My leg is a little bit sore but we must struggle on." Was that the royal we?

"What was the hospital like?"

"It was very nice, they have some very nice doctors. Your mum tells me that you've got a new boyfriend."

"He's not my boyfriend but he is ok, I've got a picture on my phone if you want to see it."

"All in good time Lucy," Jessica interjected, "Your nan is quite tired from all of this excitement. You sit down and rest your leg, mum."

"I think I might do that, dear," but before she did, she reached back into her purse to produce another ten pound note which she gave to Lucy. Quietly she whispered to the girl, "You can show me later, my sweet." The children disappeared as quick as they had arrived, no doubt already plotting how to spend their ill gotten gains.

David went out to the Jessica's car, which was crammed to the nines with luggage and all manner of things. He felt dread, how long was she staying for, even worse, perhaps she was moving in. After a while and several trips to and from the car he managed to get everything into the hall. "I will make that cup of tea now," he called into the living room, more as a reassurance to himself than to pacify the occupants. Once the kettle had boiled he dutifully asked whether Allison took sugar, he ought to know after all of these years, and then laid the tray of three cups onto the coffee table.

"We've set your bed up here, mum," Jessica explained, "and you can use the downstairs toilet out in the hall. You just make yourself at home and if there is anything you want don't be afraid to ask." David was sure that she would not be afraid to ask. "Now David you go out into the kitchen I want to talk to mum about washing facilities." Banished already and it had only been twenty minutes, still David did not need a second excuse so he grabbed his cup and in a flash he was gone.

Time passed slowly as David tinkered about the kitchen, he opened the fridge door to stare at all the contents, then looked out across the garden to see if the neighbours were up to anything, then he checked to see if the dishwasher had finished its cycle, and then finally back to the fridge to check out the contents again. He ended up sat at the kitchen table eating a chocolate bar watching the second hand go round on the kitchen clock. If my friends could see me now, he mused.

Jessica showed her face, "Everything alright, love?" she asked cautiously.

"Yeah."

"Mother has promised to try to get along and not cause too much fuss." A promise they both knew she could not keep.

David pretended to be assured, "It's only going to be for a few days I'm sure it will be fine."

Jessica kissed him on the cheek, "I know your lying but that is why I married you, you daft ape, not many men would try lie so convincingly just to keep their wives happy."

"I love you, Mrs Banks," said David, standing up to put his arms around his beloved wife so he could kiss her properly.

At that precise moment, and in that precise embrace, the kitchen door opened and there was mother, "Don't mind me," she said to the pair, "I've just come to get a glass of water for my tablets." She limped across the kitchen. David had never felt more like a naughty school-kid in all of his life, neither had Jessica, on any other day they would have probably fallen about laughing but under the circumstances it seemed better just to sit back down at the table and do nothing.

After a while they tried to settle into some sort of normal routine so Jessica went into the kitchen to prepare supper and David went into the living room to try and have a normal conversation with his mother in law. Where to begin? Stuck already, he reached for the remote control. Allison broke the ice, "How are your family, are they still living in Middlesex." David had two elder brothers both who had married and now lived abroad, but his parents did indeed still live in Middlesex. Allison had probably met his parents only once at the wedding, he was quite impressed that she remembered .

"Mum and dad still live there, my brothers they now live abroad."

"Oh yes, that's right one is an architect the other is into computers."

Where was she getting this information from? Jessica surely must have primed her with this stuff. Where was it leading, was she suggesting that her daughter had married the wrong brother. His mind whirling with mental gymnastics David could only think as far as to say, "He is an IT engineer."

"A what, dear?"

"Colin, the one that is into computers, he is an IT engineer."

"Oh that's nice."

In the same vein of casual politeness David enquired, "How long has it been since your William passed away." It was a shit question but he could not think of anything else."

"Bill...oh I think it has been just over seven years."

"My time flies, Jessica and I have been married for almost nineteen years."

"Has it really been that long, I remember it like yesterday, her father was so proud walking his daughter down the aisle."

This was like a normal conversation they were having, maybe the pain killers had mellowed her out, flushed with success David continued, "I thought she was the prettiest girl in the entire world when she walked into that church."

"Even the weather stayed nice for that one day, don't you remember, it rained the whole week before."

"Yeah, we were so worried Jessica made me buy half a dozen umbrellas to put inside the church door so the guests wouldn't get wet."

"She was always a thoughtful girl."

"She hasn't changed, we've recently adopted this stray cat."

"Does she still do that? Even when she was young she used to bring wounded animals home, it drove her father mad."

Just at that moment the former prettiest girl in the whole world entered the living room, "We're having cottage pie for tea mum, is that ok?" David gave Allison a knowing smile and she smiled back. Jessica was scared.

By early evening the truce between the two warring factions was still going strong. The children had once again been summoned from their rooms and for the first time in as long as David could remember they all ate dinner together at the dining table like any normal family. David hoped the meal would go well but feared the worst. The panacea for his worst fears was that Jessica had made a meal fit for a king, or as in this case a queen, and the children were harkened into silence buy the deliciousness of their victuals.

Nothing lasts forever. "What did they do to your knee?" asked Simon

"Not a lot dear just some repair work to the damaged cartilage."

"Are they going to amputate your leg?"

"Goodness no dear, what gave you that idea?"

"Dad said..."

"Dad never said no such thing," David interrupted. Jessica kicked him under the table. "They have such vivid imaginations at that age, I don't know where they get it from."

"How long are you staying for, are you going to be living with us?" asked Lucy.

"Did dad say that as well?" Jessica asked, giving David a look of daggers.

"Don't worry children," said the new family matriarch, "Just as soon as I am back on my feet I will be on my way."

"Now mother," said Jessica, putting on her more serious voice, "You can stay as long as you like and don't let anybody tell you any different."

"That's right," added David, partly to back his wife, and partly because he needed to dig his way out of trouble, "You stay as long as you want, we just want you to get better."

Later that evening the kids disappeared back to their bedrooms, and into the world of cyberspace, and the three adults sat down to watch television.

David suffered in silence his weekly ordeal of ballroom dancing and then was delighted to note that it would be followed by an all action thriller.

Just as the film was about to start Allison chimed in, "Does anybody mind if we turn over, only there is a lovely little documentary series I have been watching on ceramic pottery in Staffordshire."

"Of course we don't mind," said David. He minded. Half way through the documentary David pondered on the futility of life, has anybody actually died from terminal boredom watching these things, he wondered. Fully genned up on the potteries of the black country, David decided it was time for bed.

Chapter Eleven

The next day being a Sunday David was delighted to spot his neighbour about to disappear into his garden shed. Eager to escape the confines of his suburban prison he fled through the back door and over the fence. "How are you doing, Harry? Mind if I join you?"

"Not at all," said the delighted neighbour, "Step into my parlour." Harry and Jane were a retired couple, who had bought the other half of the semi-detached house, several years ago, replacing old Mr Fossett who was quietly moved into an old people's home by his family. Nobody knew whether old Mr Fossett was living or dead, but presumed dead.

Once inside the garden shed Harry closed the door and muttered, almost conspiratorially, "To tell you the truth I had to get away from it all, I am so fed up hearing about this bloody wedding. All I care about is how much it is going to bloody well cost me."

David shared his pain, "I have got the mother in law staying for God knows how long. When Jessica and her mother get together it is like being a stranger in my own home."

They both stood there shaking their heads in sympathy with one another, the world can be such a cruel place. "Fancy a cigarette?" asked Harry.

"I don't mind if I do," replied David. Harry had been forced to give up smoking many years ago after a minor cancer scare which turned out to be nothing. David had been told that he could smoke all he wanted to as long as it was not in the house, or anywhere near Jessica and the children, a situation so intolerable it was easier to give up. This was Harry and David's guilty secret, their one act of defiance that defined them as the rebels they were. Both of their wives knew exactly what they were up to in the garden shed, but allowed them this little peccadillo.

Harry reached for the secret tin he had stashed away on the top shelf, inside was an already open packet of cigarettes and a lighter.

He gave one to David and kept one for himself, and as part of their ritual he opened the sheds only window slightly ajar, and they pulled up a couple of garden chairs. They lit their illicit contraband being careful to blow their exhaled smoke out of the window. "Sometimes I don't know what I would do without our little treat," said Harry.

"I know what you mean," David concurred. They sat in silence savouring the moment.

After a while... "You are coming to the wedding aren't you," said Harry.

"Well I was going to talk to you about that," said David.

"Oh but you've got to go, you're going to be the only real friend I have there, Jane has got all of her family and Susan has got all of her friends, Gary is having a load of his friends, the only person I've got coming is my younger brother, and you know what he's like." Harry's mum and dad had died long before David had met him. Harry's brother was indeed downright weird, even by David's standards.

"Ok as long as you want us there."

"I do, I do, bring the whole family, Jane would be devastated if Jessica wasn't there."

"Jessica loves a good wedding, I don't know why because she always ends up crying. I cannot guarantee the behaviour of my kids, though."

"I am sure they'll be fine." The two men watched a bird feeding itself from the bird table in the garden. "I don't know why we have to have such an elaborate affair anyway," Harry continued. "In my day you went down the registry office, got drunk and spent the weekend in Clacton."

"We did get married in a church but we were so poor, back in those days, we had one night in a hotel and I went back to work on Monday morning."

"I blame Jane, I think because we didn't have a fairytale wedding, she wants to relive the whole thing through Susan. We had to get married in a bit of a hurry, if you know what I mean."

David knew what he meant. "When is the wedding?" he asked.

"Just under two months away."

"And is it in St Michael's church?"

"That's right, Jane will have all of the details on the invite you can be certain. Afterwards we are having a fancy meal at that posh hotel near the cemetery, and then some group and a DJ in the evening."

"Sounds lovely," said David

"Sounds expensive," said Harry, "and that is before I have laid out half the money for the bloody honeymoon."

David decided to let this be a warning of the fact that one day Lucy might decide to get married. Is it better to disown the children now and make a nice clean break of it, or should he start saving? "Doesn't the groom's family have to pay anything?" he asked, hopefully.

"Your joking aren't you, they haven't got a pot to piss in. He is a nice lad and everything but I don't think his lot have got brass farthing between them."

"Oh," David felt disheartened.

They finished their cigarettes and put them out in another secret tin Harry had stashed under his workbench full of butts. They had done this before, more times than David cared to remember. They sat and contemplated the world as the clouds rolled by. "I tell you something if this Government get their way nobody will ever be able to afford to get married ever again," said Harry.

"I know every month I seem to be paying out more and more, Jessica is thinking of getting a part time job."

"I blame the bloody banks." Everybody blamed the banks. Harry had made his fortune in the city but was still prepared to blame the banks. Just at that moment Jessica came out of the house and looked set to climb over the fence to go into next door. "Quick, duck down I think that is your wife," said Harry. Then Jane appeared at the back door to her house. "Oh my God, there's Jane now we're for it." No man likes to admit that at times they are scared of their wives, but this was not one of those times. Unified by cowardice they both ducked down and peered above the shed window ledge, like bird watchers eyeing up a rare species of fowl. Both women disappeared into the house. "Cor that was close, I thought we were done for there," said Harry.

After a while they watched as the two women reappeared at the back door and Jessica climbed over the fence back into her own domain. They waited for a while in the shed in the hope that both wives would settle down into their own domestic chores, and when they felt that their absence would no longer be tolerated the two men decided to call it a day. Certain in the knowledge that their little tryst had come to an end, they both knew that it was time to part company and return to their respective miseries.

"Maybe do this again next week," said Harry.

"That's a date," said David.

Chapter Twelve

Driving back to work on Monday morning David felt a sense of relief that he had survived the weekend, this was to the point where even being stuck in the slow moving rush hour traffic could not dampen his mood. They were playing songs on the radio that he quite liked, this truly had to be a glorious day. When he got to the office the big news was that Andrew had phoned in sick.

"But he is never ill," said Felicity. It was true, as far back as anybody could remember Andrew had never taken a day off ill in any of those years. Certainly, there had been the allocated compulsory holidays, but even then Andrew never seemed far away, he was always available by telephone or e-mail as he liked to point out constantly before such events. Thoughtful as ever, even in suffering, Andrew had sent each one of them a message to their inbox allocating certain tasks to be completed during his absence.

"What do you think it is?" asked Eric. "Do you think he's got flu or something?"

"He did say he was feeling a bit under the weather on Friday," Ronald offered.

"Maybe it is cancer," conjectured Adam.

"Don't be so stupid, you wouldn't get cancer over the weekend," said Eric, showing more restraint than Adam in an unusual turn of events. After much discussion, and surmising, the general consensus was that maybe Andrew was genuinely poorly and that is probably why he had taken the day off sick.

They were all at sea, without a captain, drifting rudderless into an ocean of God knows where. David had noticed an unusual phenomenon over the years, that during such times, instead of misbehaving as they all had the freedom to do, everybody was on their best behaviour settling down and working harder than as if Andrew was there to keep a beady eye on them. This was less out of respect to Andrew, as a great leader, but more out of an inability to know what to do otherwise. Maybe they had lost their referee if things got out of control, so they were afraid to let things get out of control.

"Could you pass me last week's time-sheets?" David asked Ronald, more cordially than a distinguished gentleman at a dinner party. It felt like they were in an old black and white movie.

"Certainly dear boy," Ronald responded, all but forgetting to polish his monocle.

"Has anybody seen the stapler?" asked Eric.

Everybody rushed to help. "Here it is," said Felicity, dutifully obliging. Everybody pretended not to notice the unedifying tension in the air, nobody wanted to admit to missing their obsequious superior. It was as if they were knights of the round table without one of their knights. It felt wrong and nobody would be able to put their finger on why it felt wrong, but it just did.

By the time dinner arrived it was a blessed relief. Everybody had been so stultifyingly nice to each other that it was beginning to hurt. There was a staff canteen which some people chose to use, others brought their own sandwiches, and the rest tended to disappear off for an hour. Today David went for the canteen option, the food was pleasant enough, if not a little bit greasy, with reasonable prices. The hardest part of eating in the canteen was choosing who to sit with, if you were not careful you could be caught in the awkward situation of having to sit with somebody you did not particularly like, rather than sit on your own. The best way around this was to take somebody from the office with you, and then you were guaranteed your own little clique circle that acted as a buffer against unwanted strays. David took Eric and Adam with him for safety.

"What happened with your date over the weekend?" David asked Adam, "Did it go well?" He waited for Eric to ask the obligatory, "Did you shag her?" and was surprised when it did not come.

"Actually," said Adam, "we had a really nice time. A really, really nice time." Still Eric did not interject with the "Did you shag her?" question, maybe he was catching Andrew's illness. David was so thrown that he almost had to ask Adam himself.

"Where did you go, what did you do?" David continued.

"Well I took her to the cinema on Friday, and then on Saturday we just went out for a couple of drinks."

"Wait a minute," said David, "So you went out with her twice over the weekend," with the emphasis on the word 'twice'.

"Yes," said Adam.

"Did you shag her?" David had to ask, he could stand Eric's silence no more.

"She's not that kind of a girl," Adam replied, "She is more decent than the other slags."

"I'd have shagged her," at last Eric woke up, "There's no point going out with her if you can't get a decent shag out of it."

David pretended not to hear Eric, "So you really like her then?"

"Well it is early days but she messaged her friend to say that she thought I was really cute."

"You had better watch out Adam," said David with a smile, "You never know this time she could be the one."

They finished their dinner with the contentment of the knowledge that they just might have stumbled upon something here.

After dinner the tension in the office seemed to have eased. There is life after Andrew they must have decided. Now if anybody asked for the stapler they would get the mandatory, "look for it yourself, you had it last" response.

"Adam is in love," Eric told the rest of the office not privy to their lunchtime conversation.

"Adam went beetroot exacerbated by the fact that he looked even redder under his bleach blonde hair. "I did not...I never..." he spluttered. Everybody laughed.

"Your secret is out now," Felicity said to him mischievously.

"Well I for one am very pleased for the lad," said Ronald. "Don't you let them tease you boy, you just make the most of it."

"Do you want to see a picture?" Adam asked Ronald, knowing that the whole office would want to have a look. "I think I have got it here on my mobile phone." After a while Adam managed to find the picture he wanted on the phone. Everybody crowded round eager to get a glimpse of the new Mona Lisa.

"She's lovely," said Felicity, "What is her name?" She was beginning to sound like she was looking at a new born baby, an analogy David always felt uncomfortable with around Felicity.

"Cadenza," replied Adam, "I think one of her parents is Spanish or something."

"She's fit," said Eric, "You want to get in there, boy," most likely a reference to the 'shagging' conversation of earlier. "It's a pity that we can't quite see her knockers." Careful Eric, remember Andrew is not here to stop you now.

"I told you before, she is not that kind of a girl," said Adam defensively, switching off the mobile phone and shoving it in his pocket contemptuously.

"Don't worry, Adam, I am only having a laugh with you." Perhaps Eric had suddenly remembered Andrew's absence.

Excitement over they all went back to their jobs, the knights of the Harman and Cooke Insurance Agency vowing to fight on without their beloved leader.

Chapter Thirteen

After work when David arrived home he could not wait to tell Jessica all about Andrew's absence. Having got through the front door he thought it prudent to knock on the door to the living room, less out of politeness, and more out of the thought of how traumatised his mind would be if he accidentally caught his mother in law in a state of semi-undress.

"Come in," said the voice within. The absurdity of having to knock on his own door, in his own house did not escape David. Inside Allison was propped up in the bed, in semi-darkness, surrounded by an array of assorted objects. She was watching some sort of late afternoon detective drama on the television with the volume up way too loud.

"Where's Jessica?" David shouted to be heard.

"I think she is in the kitchen, "came the reply.

David retraced his steps and went into the kitchen. Jessica was sat at the kitchen table, it looked like she had been reading a magazine. "Hello love," David said to her, "You will never guess who took the day off sick today." Jessica looked up. At this point David suddenly noticed that her eyes were all red and puffy and his train of thought instantly lost him, "Have you been crying?" he exclaimed. At moments like this David loved her even more and he wanted to cherish and protect her from all of the evils of this world. "Has your mum done something to upset you?" Silence. "Has she been running you ragged, or something?"

"No it is not that." It was that, thought David. "I just want to try to help mum as best I can but, you know what she is like, she is so fiercely independent she won't let me do a thing for her. She is just like dad, he was the same and look what happened to him." Jessica burst into a fresh set of tears, uncontrollably sobbing.

David put his arms around her, "Look if she won't accept our help then we will just have to make her. I know you want to help her, love, but I guess she has lived on her own for so long it is probably difficult for her to accept any sort of aid." When did David get his degree in psychiatry? "You cannot compare her to what happened to your dad, that was a different thing altogether," continued Dr David Banks MD, "she is not going to die, she just wants to keep her independence." For some unknown reason David wanted to phone his parents right there, right then and tell them how much he loved them.

Jessica looked at David through tear stained eyes. "But you don't even like her," she strained a smile, "and that is why I love you Mr Banks."

David smiled back, "I love you too, Mrs Banks. I might decide to kill her when she gets better," he quipped, "but I don't want her dead body cluttering up the living room just yet." They hugged each other for a long while and David felt like it was them versus the world.

Later that evening when everybody had eaten and the kids had disappeared once more into their rooms, (where did they go, maybe it was Narnia), Jessica and her mum had settled down to watch the soaps so David decided to give his parents a call. He took the cordless telephone into the kitchen and dialled the number which Jessica had programmed into the device. His mum answered.

"Hi mum, I was just calling to see how you were."

"Hello, David," his mother sounded quite jovial, "Funny enough I was just talking about you to your father." Serendipity.

"How are you keeping? How's Colin and Peter, have you heard from them at all?" David asked.

"Colin and Peter are fine."

"Colin and Peter are fine. Are you and dad ok?"

"Yeah we're ok, we've been busy here getting the kitchen done."

"Oh, you're having the kitchen done, are you mum?"

"Well what with the fire and everything."

"The fire..." David was aware that he was repeating everything she said, but with the shock and everything he could not stop himself. "What fire?"

"Well after the kitchen burnt down we thought it was a good excuse to put in whole new fitted units."

"The kitchen burnt down," repeated Mr Slater's parrot. "What the Hell happened?"

"Oh it was nothing, your father left the ring on. The fire brigade said it could have been a lot worse. It was mostly the smoke and the water that caused a lot of the damage."

David started to wonder if he was dreaming, "Mum your house caught fire and you didn't think to tell me."

"Well we didn't want to worry you."

"You didn't want to worry me," Polly syndrome had returned. "Right mum, we have got Jessica's mother staying at the moment but just as soon as she is gone I am coming straight over to visit."

"Oh that would be nice dear, bring the grandchildren. The kitchen should be finished by then, it looks lovely."

"Bye, mum, say hello to dad for me."

"Bye, David, give my love to Jessica and the children."

David was in shock. He listened to the dialling tone of the receiver and stared at the instrument as though it gave you a direct line to the gateway of Hell. Impulsively he decided to phone Peter, what time was it in New Zealand, anyway? Being eight years older than David, David had always looked to his elder brother for approval growing up. Nothing he did seemed ever good enough for Peter, but when David did earn his praise it felt like manna from Heaven. When David and Jessica got married, secretly he hoped that Peter would be able to attend the wedding. Everybody told him that Peter was in New Zealand and it would be too far for him to come but David clung on to a glimmer of hope anyway. Even when they were showing him and Jessica a video filmed before the wedding congratulating them on their big day, David still kind of expected Peter to burst through the door shouting "surprise." The resentment ran deep but that was a long time ago and he was over it now, or so David thought.

After a long while Peter answered the phone, "Hello."

David instantly recognised the voice, "Did you know that mum and dad's house practically burnt to the ground?" he asked accusingly, forgetting all of the formalities of politeness in his anger.

"Uh...David I don't know what time it is in the UK but it is eight o'clock in the morning over here."

"Well did you?" asked David.

There was a pause and then Peter replied, "The house did not burn to the ground they had a small kitchen fire that is all."

"So you knew?"

"Dad mentioned it in an e-mail he sent me. What does it matter?"

"You knew and you didn't think to tell me."

"I thought that you already knew. Christ, David, it was hardly the Great Fire of London."

"So mum and dad practically dying in their beds is no big deal to you, then?"

"Here we go again, you have always been the same even as a little kid, overdramatizing everything." Peter could always pull rank as the eldest child it never failed.

"Well I just think you should have let me know," said David petulantly.

"Well I will be sure to let you in on every detail of their lives in future," said Peter with more than a little degree of sarcasm. After a while, "Anyway, how are Jessica and the kids?"

"They are fine," David mellowed, "Is Wendy alright, and the twins are they OK?"

"Wendy has got a new job teaching in a primary school, Tom and Nancy, well you should see them they are growing up so fast."

"I know what you mean, you wouldn't hardly recognise Lucy and Simon." Not unless they regressed back to infancy and climbed in their cots. Come to think about it, had Peter ever seen Simon in the flesh at all? Why did his brother have to emigrate so far?

"I bet they must be teenagers now, I think Lucy is only a couple of years younger than the twins."

"When are you coming back to the UK for a visit, Pete?"

"Not this year, but maybe soon."

"Ok, look forward to it." They parted friends. They both agreed that they must e-mail each other more often, but they knew deep down that they never would.

After he had hung up, David in a more sober mood, decided to call his other brother in Spain. Colin and David had grown up with a much closer age gap, of only one year, so they were more like best friends than brothers. The phone took less time to answer this time around, it was Colin's girlfriend, what was her name again? David racked his brain but for the life of him he could not remember. "Is Colin there?" he asked, sounding dumb.

"I will just get him for you," said the mystery voice, "Can I ask who is calling?"

"Tell him it is his brother, David."

"David, I hardly recognised your voice over the phone. How are you, is everything alright?"

"Yeah, fine, I just need to chat to Colin about something that's all." Still her name would not come.

"Sure." David heard the sound of the receiver being dropped and then distantly he heard, "Colin your brother is on the phone."

"What does he want?" he heard his brother's faded voice.

There was the sound of somebody picking up the phone. David could only presume it was Colin, "Nice to hear from you too..." he said with polite cynicism.

"Davey boy," It was a testament to the closeness of their relationship that Colin could speak to him in the same way as his best friend Mark. "What is the matter, is anything wrong?"

"Why does everyone assume that just because I call them something is wrong?" everyone being Colin and his as yet unnamed girlfriend.

"It is just unusual, that is all." Colin put up a half-hearted defence.

"I was calling to find out if you had heard about the fire at mum and dad's place."

"Yeah the kitchen burnt down, terrible business they were very lucky."

Did everybody know? They might as well have put an advert in the local paper, 'House Burns Down In Middlesex' with the byline of, 'Don't Tell David'. "Why didn't you tell me," his tone was far less accusery than it was with his eldest brother Peter.

"I thought you knew, to be honest."

"They never told me," David bleated.

"I expect they didn't want to worry you."

With all of the bases covered it felt natural to move on to other topics. "How is life in Spain?"

"Beautiful, you know you can come out and see us anytime."

"I would but we have already booked a holiday down in Cornwall this year," David lied, deciding there and then to take Mark up on his offer.

"Oh that is such a shame, you would love it here. Are you going down to see Mark?"

"Yeah, hopefully."

"Tell him he still owes me a toy soldier," Colin laughed. It was an old joke but it brought back memories of their childhood.

David laughed too, "I expect him to post it First Class, it is only about thirty years too late."

There was a pause and then Colin said, "Well, I guess I will see you around." A phrase that obviously did not apply, the chances of David taking a plane overseas and then happen to bump into his brother, who was luckily wandering around the same Spanish village and at the same time were certainly negligible.

"Yeah, see you around," David resisted the urge to ask Colin what was the name of his girlfriend, after all the pair had only been together now for at least ten years. Jessica would know.

Chapter Fourteen

A couple of days later David and Jessica were in the car driving to the school to keep an appointment which Jessica had arranged with Simon's headmaster. They were still none the wiser as to why they had been summoned but duty calls.

They had left the children at home, watered and fed, and with strict instructions not to pester their grandmother. As they drove towards the school, in the early evening traffic, they made polite conversation.

"Andrew still hasn't come back to work yet, it's been three days," David informed Jessica.

"Maybe he has got that stomach virus, there is a lot of it around," said Jessica, "Mrs Webber from across the way had it for three weeks."

"I don't think we could last three weeks without him at the office. It's funny isn't it how you miss these people when they are not there."

"You normally don't like the guy."

"Yeah, that's true," David laughed. He watched the world going by and then felt compelled to ask, "When you booked the appointment are you sure that they did not give a hint or a clue about what it is all about."

"No."

"And they didn't say he was being bullied."

"I told you, David, I only spoke to the secretary. Stop going on about it we will find out when we get there, it's like this bloody fire..." The mood in the car was starting to darken.

"I guess you are right, love, it surely can't be that bad."

Jessica was adjusting her make-up in the passenger mirror. "Actually," she said, softened her tone, "it feels a bit weird being called to the headmaster's office, it makes you feel like you have done something wrong in school."

"I know what you mean," David chortled, "I am a forty-three years old and I still feel like a disobedient schoolboy."

They arrived at the school gates. "There's plenty of parking spaces," David observed, "we must be the only ones, here." What had he expected a cavalcade of motor vehicles.

The naughty children went back to school, through the double doors and up to the window of the reception area. There was a prettier than expected woman sitting behind the glass, she slid the pane across, "Can I help you?" she enquired.

"Yes, it is Mr and Mrs Banks here to see Mr...Mr..." David looked to his wife.

"Mr Chilcott," Jessica spared his blushes.

"Certainly," said the pretty secretary, "His office is just down the corridor on the left, I will let him know you are here."

They followed the corridor as instructed until they got to a door with the austere words 'Mr Chilcott School Governor' on it. There were some plastic chairs outside the room, and David wondered how many children had sat on them in nervous anticipation before, come to think about it, how many parents too.

They sat and waited. "Do you think we are going to get the cane?" David asked his wife.

"Only if you are a good boy later," Jessica whispered.

"Thank you, Miss." David responded, half tempted to playfully fondle her breast.

The door opened and out stepped a rather tall man with a large nose. "Mr and Mrs Banks," he smiled, "My name is Mr Chilcott," he offered to shake their hands.

Well at least we have all managed to identify each other, David thought, as he shook the man's hand.

The man bode them into his office and ushered them to a couple of chairs, then he went behind his desk and sat down. He picked up a pair of glasses and appeared to be perusing some paperwork on his desk, and then he started looking at his computer screen.

This is all very formal, thought David.

"Ah it is about your son, Simon." said the headmaster.

I could have told you that, thought David. David looked at the man and slowly began to realise that he had a spot on the end of his very large proboscis. Why does nature do that, he thought to himself, it always seems to draw attention to any physical abnormality in some sort of perverse sense of sod's law.

"Simon is a very gifted boy, in fact, it seems he is nearly top of the class in every subject." David found himself transfixed by the spot on the man's nose. "I have his reports here in front of me and the only subject he appears to be lacking in is physical education."

"He doesn't like sports," David heard Jessica say, "He is a very delicate child."

"Hhhmm," said the man behind the desk, "be that as it may the school has a very strict policy on sports education." As David stared the spot seemed to grow and grow, to the point where it had now covered the whole of the man's face. "But that is not why I have asked you to come here, today, I wanted to talk to you on a more personal level."

David did not like where this was going.

"Does Simon have very many friends, either in school or at home?" asked the spot. "In my opinion the boy is a very insular child, have you considered engaging him in activities of a more social nature like canoeing, or after school clubs?"

Inside David's head he wanted to tell the headmaster that they had not asked for a so called 'gifted' child, and that they would be quite happy to trade him in for one that plays football and chases girls, but all that came out of his mouth was, "We have tried to get him interested in after school events but he prefers to read books."

"Yes, I have reports that say he likes to stay indoors and read during the breaktimes," said the ever expanding spot.

David could stand it no more, "Mr Chilcott, do you think our son is being bullied?" He did not need to be telepathic to know that Jessica was thinking angry thoughts towards him.

"No, no, not that we are aware of," ventured the headmaster, and then looking confused added, "Is there something that the school should know about?"

Jessica brought sanity to the proceedings, "Mr Chilcott, my husband is just concerned that being different from the other children might stigmatise our son."

"And that is exactly why I brought you in here. I know that being the parents of a very gifted child can be a difficult experience." What do you know, I bet you have not got one, thought David. "But there are certain groups who can help, in fact, I have drawn up a list of internet sites where you can talk to other parents in exactly the same situation." The teacher passed Jessica a piece of paper with a load of information on it. "Also, if you want, I can arrange to for the boy to talk to one of our specially trained counsellors. Would you like me to do that?"

David breathed a sigh of relief, "Oh it's ok, Simon isn't going to commit suicide, I asked him."

"You asked him?"

"Yes."

"You asked your son if he was going to commit suicide?"

"That's right." Why is everybody looking at me, David wondered, I am not the one with a massive great zit on the end of my nose.

"Why would you do that?" asked an astonished headmaster. David felt like he was in the dock.

"Because of the programme." Ladies and gentlemen of the jury there is no need for you to retire...

"What programme?"

"The one on the television," even as he said it sounded puerile. David wondered if they would even make it home before social services took the children away.

Mr Chilcott turned to Jessica as though she were the only sane person in the room, "Mrs Banks I strongly urge you to get in touch with some of the contact addresses I have just given you." He then turned to David, "Mr Banks I can assure you that our only concern is for Simon's well being is his inability to integrate with the other children. Perhaps he needs more intellectual stimulation than the other pupils can give him, this is why I suggest counselling, to find out what is best for Simon, no other reason."

"Sounds great to me," squeaked the admonished schoolboy once known as David Banks.

"So you would like me to book Simon a counsellor?"

David and Jessica acted grateful. "That would be nice, thank you very much," they muttered in unison. Punishment accepted, can we go home now, thought David.

The spot would not let up, "If you really are having trouble, I have written down my personal telephone number, please feel free to talk to me any time of the day or night." An idea which horrified David beyond recognition, suddenly he had the mischievous impulse to phone the headmaster at three in the morning.

"Thanks, once again," David pretended to really care.

Then it was over, the headmaster stood up and they all shook hands and everybody went home.

"That went well," David said to Jessica as they were driving back, and felt that the silence emanating from the passenger seat was a bad omen. "I am in trouble, aren't I?" he asked. Never was a truer word spoken by any man.

Chapter Fifteen

Friday afternoon and all of the people at the office had survived whole week without Andrew. David treated himself by nosing what self catering holidays were available in Cornwall on the internet. After much searching he found a lovely little cottage in the heart of the West Country, not too far from where Mark and his family lived, and only seven hundred and eighty pounds a week. Considering the amount, and their forever dwindling savings, he decided not to broach Jessica with the idea of spending their summer vacation in Cornwall quite yet.

With a stack of work still to catch up on before the weekend David decided to go for the, 'fuck it let's leave it 'til Monday' option rather than bog himself down with a heavy workload. Everybody else in the office was equally busy, he could see Adam looking at the latest Ferrari online and over his shoulder Eric nosing internet porn. Ronald was composing a letter to his bank manager and Felicity, what the Hell was Felicity doing?

"What the Hell are you doing Felicity?" it seemed easier to ask than try to guess.

"I am looking at this new dating site, where men can post pictures of their private parts for everybody else to look at. It cuts out all the faffing around, you know exactly what you are getting, saves wasting time." On the screen were several photographs of men's genitalia.

David felt physically sick. "People actually go on dates from this site."

"Yes, why waste time spending ages trying to get to know somebody and, just when you are starting to like them, discovering they are not very blessed in the lower regions, shall we say."

We truly live in modern times, thought David. "Have you been on one of these dates?" and then he started to regret asking the question.

"Not yet but I have got a few potential candidates," Felicity replied, candidly. David was astonished that she could talk about this as though she were buying a packet of frozen peas from the supermarket.

"Let's have a look," said Eric wheeling his chair over. "Cor I wouldn't bother with him, Felicity," he said laughing, "He couldn't satisfy a mouse."

David wondered if he was dreaming this. Adam and Rodney were becoming interested so they all gathered around Felicity's computer analysing photographs of naked men from the waist down.

"That one looks bent up," said Adam.

"Yeah, and that one looks positively weird," said Rodney.

Before he knew it David found himself joining in the fun, "That one has got a metal bar going through it, my God that is disgusting."

"And that one there would frighten an elephant, let alone a human being," said Rodney. "And there is one with a tattoo on it, is that even legal?"

"Look at that one with the leather strap round it," said Eric. Everyone looked and it felt great they had not had a day at the office where everybody was in a good mood for a very long time. Too long, in fact, they bonded together over the screen staring at men's scrotums, laughing out loud and genuinely having fun.

After a while they wiped the tears from their eyes, chatted about things in general, and sent Adam off to get them coffee. "Why is it always me that has to go," he whined, but he was expected to moan and it almost added to the sense of fun. Adam himself could not stop himself smiling even as he bitched about it and compliantly disappeared off to do his duty.

They talked about their plans for the weekend, which were mostly dependant on the weather, they wondered whether or not Andrew would be back on Monday, and generally chit-chatted about things in general. Inevitably, as it always does when conversation runs out, they ended up discussing what they would do if they won the lottery. Listening to other people talking about what they would do with their lottery winnings, to David, was a bit like listening to somebody

74

telling you what they dreamt about last night, it was probably nice if you were there but dead boring for the rest of the world.

"Money is not all it is cracked up to be," said Ronald. You should know, thought David. "When you have got it everybody wants it, you spend most of your time worrying about keeping it. Money changes everything. I tell you I am better off now than I was then."

"But don't you miss the fancy restaurants and the fast cars?" Eric asked him.

"No not really once you have eaten at one Hilton you have done them all. As far as the fast cars go I spent most of my time in the back of the Bentley stuck in slow moving traffic."

Eric would not give up, "But I bet you had loads of celebrity friends and wild parties you could go to."

"Yes, I surely had loads of friends," Ronald confirmed, "But I can tell you when the money ran out they disappeared as fast as greased lightning. If you want the truth I consider you lot to be the best friends that I ever had."

"You don't mean that," said Eric, "Not our sad lot."

"I do, I really do," Ronald continued, "You lot are more loyal and trustworthy to me than any of those greedy pigs with their snouts in the trough up at head office." It gave everyone in the office a warm glow inside.

"What, even Adam?" Eric inquired, jokingly.

"Even Adam," Ronald laughed.

At that time the poignancy of these words were lost on David for this was a conversation that David found himself replaying over and over again in his head. Who could have known that this would be the last time they would ever see Ronald alive on earth. No living person can predict when the number of their days are up, and nobody could have known that Ronald's days were at an end. Unbeknown to the people laughing and joking in Harman and Cooke's finest Region 28 office, Ronald was to go home and suffer a heart attack from which he sadly would never recover.

In future times David would look back at this conversation with the fond memories that only death can create. Famous people had uttered last words that were witty and pithy and would go down in history but sadly for Ronald the only words that David could remember were, 'Even Adam.' It comforted David, and everyone else at the office, that the last day they had spent with Ronald had been full of fun and frivolity. Who could dare ask for more than that as their time on planet earth dwindled to an end?

Chapter Sixteen

None of the forthcoming events were known to David when he reached home that Friday evening, so he was still in an upbeat buoyant mood when he arrived back at the house. Even the thought of spending another weekend with the mother-in-law could not dampen his good mood. Cell mates with the most ferocious animosity towards each other eventually give in and start talking at some point. David was whistling a tune he had heard on the radio when he entered the kitchen where Jessica and her mum were sat drinking coffee.

"You are in a good mood, love," said Jessica.

"Actually I had a really good day at the office" David confirmed.

"Oh really what happened that made it such a good day?" asked Jessica. "Did Andrew come back or something?"

"No Andrew was still off, but we spent the afternoon looking at...looking at...well Felicity..." it slowly dawned on David the company he was in. "Never mind we just had a great day, besides it's the weekend and I get to spend it with my two favourite people," he said, kissing Jessica on the cheek. David knew it was a lie but it did not hurt sometimes.

"Mum and I have been talking too," said Jessica, "and she has got some great news she wants to tell you." She has had enough of us and she wants to go back to her house straight away, thought David. That would be an excellent day. "Tell him, mum."

Allison actually looked embarrassed, "You tell him," she said to her daughter.

"Mum has given us a thousand pounds for letting her stay here."

Truly the Gods were shining their light on David, "That's great Allison but we cannot possibly accept it," he said, all the while thinking 'yes, we can'.

"Now I will not hear another word about it," said Allison, "When Jessica's father died, God rest his soul, he had a considerable life insurance policy, so helping out my family once in a while is the least I can do."

I wonder how much the old girl is worth? David considered committing murder for the first time in his life. It seemed Ronald was right money did change everything. "Well if you insist, and we can't change your mind, "he said. Inside his head David was already plotting how to spend the money on a summer vacation down in Cornwall with the children. Winning Jessica over to the idea might be difficult, it would be a matter of finding the right moment, at the right place and the right time but it could be done.

David decided to have a shower and put on a fresh set of clothes before supper, life had never felt so good.

Later the next day Allison was in the front room watching some black and white movie, way too loud, that seemed to have lots of explosions in it. Jessica and David had done the shopping and were putting it away, the children had disappeared to God knows where, for neither of them were in their rooms, and David knew this was his chance to broach the idea of going down to Cornwall for a holiday. "Jessica," he said, "You know I love you, don't you."

"Yes," she replied, cautiously.

"And I love the children more than anything else on earth."

"Yes," Jessica's suspicions were really aroused now.

"I've been thinking..."

"Thinking what?"

"Why don't we use the extra cash your mother has given us to book a holiday down in Cornwall?"

Silence.

"We could go and see Mark, and you like his girlfriend, and they have got a little toddler called Zig, or something. Plus, it might be the last chance we all get to have a holiday as a family together, what with Lucy and Simon growing up so fast."

Jessica looked lost in thought, David waited anxiously for her reaction, time passed then eventually, "Ok yeah, I agree...let's do it."

"Let's do what?"

"Let's book a holiday down in Cornwall."

David was thrown sideways he had so many plausible reasons why they should go to level at her that he lost his bearings. In this confused state he started to argue her side for her. "But you know it costs a lot of money to go on holiday."

"Yes."

"And it is a Hell of a drive."

"Yes."

"And the kids will probably play up every step of the way."

"Yes."

"So why do you want to go?"

"Because, like you said, it will probably be the last thing we do as a family. What good is having all this extra cash if we don't make the most of it."

David hugged her and hugged her some more, he was afraid to let go in case she was transformed into some ugly old harridan, and not the beautiful understanding wife God had blessed him with. Eventually he had to let her go for fear that all of the frozen stuff would melt all over the floor if they did not put it in the freezer.

Shopping all stacked away they got the laptop out sat down with two mugs of tea at the kitchen table. Jessica typed 'Holiday Cottages In Cornwall' into the search engine. They spent what felt like hours going through place after place until they finally settled on one that they both agreed with. It was a converted barn set among a conclave of other converted barns, it had three bedrooms and wi-fi to keep the children happy, on top of which it was only a short drive from the coast, and not a million miles away from where Mark lived.

"This is the one," David declared.

"I think you are right," Jessica agreed. David decided to let Jessica pick up the phone because she was the better negotiator than he was, and after some hard bargaining on her part Jessica got them two weeks late August for under seven hundred quid. And then it was done, David looked at Jessica and she stared back and they were suddenly committed. "Let's break the good news to mother," said Jessica, if only to break the awkwardness.

"Yes, let's," David felt it too.

Jessica's mother was delighted, "Oh I think that is a wonderful idea and so thoughtful of you Jessica," she said. David was about to protest that it was his idea but decided against rocking the boat, and then for an awful moment he started to wonder if she thought she was coming with them.

"Thanks mum, you are the best," said Jessica.

"And don't you forget to send me a postcard," said Allison. Panic over David almost audibly breathed a sigh of relief.

They left Jessica's mother to carry on watching her afternoon movie, and went back into the kitchen to look at what had now become their barn, on the internet. "That was the easy part," said Jessica, "next comes the hard bit, telling the children."

First through the door was Simon. "Where have you been?" David enquired.

"Just to get a couple of things for my science project," the boy replied. Most parents would probably be pleased that their son was showing an interest in science, David worried that their son might be creating new life, or a bomb, or who knows what he was getting up to.

"That's nice," said Jessica, but even her face looked like she was worried about the safety of the house. "Your father and I have got some exciting news to tell you. We are going to Cornwall for two weeks in August, isn't that great."

"Do we have to?" asked Simon.

"I'm afraid so." David stepped in.

"What if I don't want to go?" Simon asked, hope dying in his eyes.

"Tough," said his dad.

"Have they got the internet in Cornwall?" Simon continued his questioning.

David threw down his ace card, "Yes, the place we are staying at has got wi-fi."

"Thank God for small mercies, still sounds 'trick' if you ask me," said the boy as he disappeared out the kitchen door.

"That was the easy one," said David to Jessica.

Jessica agreed, "One down, one to go," she said with a sigh.

Eventually Lucy showed her face at the kitchen door, it was getting late, dinner was almost ready.

"Where have you been?" it was Jessica's turn to ask.

"Me and Jack went to the cinema," she replied.

"Did you see anything good?" Jessica kept it light.

"No it was a bit boring, really," Lucy replied.

"Anyway sit down we have got something to tell you," said Jessica. They broke the news to their daughter about Cornwall.

She took it well. "I hate you. How could you do this to me? I hate you," she screamed, "I am not going," she shouted at them between floods of tears.

"You are going and that's that," said Jessica, always the final arbiter of all things serious, "Besides they have got wi-fi you can still stay in touch with all of your friends."

"This morsel of comfort was completely lost on Lucy, "Don't blame me if I end up killing myself," she screamed at them, as flew out of the kitchen and off to her bedroom to tell the entire internet what cruel parents she had.

"I think that went better than expected," said David, in the silence of the aftermath.

"She will probably calm down," Jessica hoped.

Allison peered around the kitchen door, "Is everything ok?" she asked, tentatively.

"Yeah, we just broke the news to Lucy about Cornwall," said Jessica.

"Oh," was all Allison could say.

Chapter Seventeen

Going back to work on Monday morning was almost a blessed relief for David. The house was like a mausoleum with the children sulking over their enforced holiday, the tension was definitely rife. Unusually he was the first to arrive at the office and unexpectedly the first face that he saw coming through the door was Andrew's.

"Hi Andrew, are you feeling any better," David asked of him.

"Yes, I think it was one of those stomach bugs, or something," Andrew replied.

Andrew still looked very green around the gills. David forced himself to say, "Well I am glad that you are back." After all it was only a partial lie.

The others arrived, ensemble, all apart from Ronald, and made their reparations as to how well Andrew was looking and how much they had missed him. David wondered if Andrew believed a word of it or perhaps he was so glad to be alive it took it all at face value.

By ten o'clock tea break the office was awash with gossip about where the hell Ronald could be.

"He must have caught the same bug as you," said Felicity, and everyone agreed as it seemed the most plausible explanation.

"Still it seems strange that he has not phoned in sick," said Andrew, ever the pedant.

After a while Andrew who had been looking worried most of the morning interrupted their coffee-break reverie. "I am glad that I've got you all here," he said to the four of them, "While I was away I received a memo from head office which is rather concerning me." Everyone was intrigued. "It seems even though the company's profits are up for the first two financial quarters of this year, they want to make some changes and that involves streamlining every department." Nobody liked where this was going. "So the long and the short of it is," Andrew wriggled like a worm on a hook, "that we have to lose a member of our team."

Everybody looked shocked. They did what any decent set of human beings would do when faced with such adversity, they turned on each other.

Eric started the ball rolling, "Well I think that Ronald should go, he is the oldest."

David interjected, "But I don't think they can fire him, I think he has a special contract. All I know is that he has something big on some of the head cheeses and they probably won't dare to mess with him."

Andrew felt forced to say, "Nobody has ever said anything to me about that."

"You go then," said Eric to David.

"But I've got a wife and family to support, besides we are going to Cornwall this summer," he offered in mitigation.

"Adam should go," said Felicity, "last in first out." Everyone looked at Adam.

"I am afraid it doesn't work that way anymore," Andrew offered the voice of reason.

"I can't go I need this job, I've got a new girlfriend," said Adam. "You should go Felicity, you're the only woman here, you don't even have a partner."

"But I am the only woman here, that is why I should stay," Felicity retaliated. "What about you Eric, maybe you should look for a new job."

"I can't, not now, things have changed," Eric replied, "I wasn't going to tell you lot this, not yet, not until we were sure, but seeing as you have forced my hand, Lola is expecting a baby."

Everybody looked sheepish and stared at the floor as they all mumbled their congratulations.

Andrew stamped his authority as boss, "Look nothing has been decided yet. I will have to go over the details with Mr Dixon and we might come up with a solution that is mutually beneficial for everyone concerned. Let's not worry for the moment, let's wait and see." Everybody was worried, as a motivational speech it flopped on every level.

By lunchtime each member of the office saw every other member as a potential enemy. Harman and Cooke's team bonding exercises of two years ago had completely gone out of the window. They all sat together in the staff canteen, less out of kinsmanship and more out of fear of being the one talked about if not there.

"Well I think we should all storm out of the office and tell them we are all going on strike," said Eric, with false bravado.

"They'll probably fire us all and move the office to Norfolk," said Felicity, dashing his dreams. The Norfolk branch over the years had become their arch enemy, region 28's nemesis.

"Perhaps we should ask Ronald what it is he has got on them and then we could blackmail them." David threw his pennyworth into the pot.

"Get real," said Eric, the man who had just suggested walking out, "Like that is ever going to happen."

"Well have you got a better plan?" asked David.

"Adam you should quit." Eric knifed his fellow brother in arms.

"Fuck off, Eric, I have got just as much right to be here as you."

"So have you got a baby on the way, then?" Eric demanded, folding his arms.

"No but I am better at my job than you," Adam stomped his feet.

Felicity could stand it no more and showed her true colours as the only humanitarian of the group, "I'll go," she said to a stunned audience, "If the worst comes to the worst I will put my name down as the one to go."

She did not deserve to lose that baby, thought David. They all sat in astounded silence. For the first time in their lives Eric and Adam had nothing to say.

Nothing lasts forever. "Why should you be the one to fall on your sword?" asked Eric.

"I thought you would be pleased," Felicity answered, "Besides maybe it is time for me to move on start a new life." Brave and humanitarian, David was starting to see Felicity in a new light.

"Well I don't think you should be the one to go," said Eric, glaring at Adam.

There would be no sending out for coffee and doughnuts this afternoon, David mused as he sat at his computer. Still stunned from Felicity's unwarranted act of kindness he pondered over each member of the team. They were right that Adam was the new boy, and he never had to sit in that freezing river, but he was so damn likable and he was always compliant about getting tea's or sandwiches, or whatever. Eric could be brusque and had an attitude but he was honest, and even though he and David had had some run-ins you knew where you stood with Eric, besides the baby thing really did count for something. Nobody understood Ronald except David, David got him and he got David, it is a rare thing in life where you can understand someone on a tacit level, those friendships should always be treasured. And what about Felicity, the mother of the group, hardworking, maternal, often the one to settle disputes and reinstall harmony, she had been elevated to new heights in David's world. Damn it, she cannot go David resolved inside his head, there must be another way. He decided there and then to work on the problem.

Chapter Eighteen

By the time David arrived home that evening inside his mind he had exaggerated events out of all proportions. "Guess what, I have been fired," he told a gobsmacked Jessica, who nearly dropped her lasagne on the floor.

"You what," she almost choked.

"Well all but..." David went on to explain everything that Andrew had said.

"For God's sake, David, you had me really worried there for a moment," Jessica berated him. "They are obviously not going to fire you. Didn't you tell me that only the other day Andrew was looking at you as his replacement?"

"Well somebody has got to go," said David, defensively, "No job is safe these days."

"I know but I am sure that Andrew will make the right decision," said Jessica ever the pragmatist.

"In other news," said David, "Ronald never showed up for work today, and Eric and Lolita are pregnant. Well she is, if you know what I mean."

This was almost information overload for Jessica who was used to David coming home and telling her that the office pot plant had died or, as in the other day, the occasional office bust-up. As usual Jessica took it all in her stride, after all she had lived with David for far too long. She decided to change the subject. "I think that the kids are getting more used to the idea of going on holiday," she said. She probably means Lucy, thought David. "Some of Lucy's friends told her that going to Newquay was really cool, so she has calmed down a lot." She did mean Lucy.

It had taken David this long to realise that something was amiss and then suddenly he put his finger on it, "Where's your mother," he asked, only this time there was no underlying subtext of wishing she was dead. Maybe she had grown on him.

"I dropped her off at the local hospital, she is getting her knee checked and her dressings changed," Jessica replied, "She said that afterwards she was going to take a taxi into town. Come to think of it that was hours ago, I had better give her a ring." Jessica phoned her mother's mobile, no answer. "She is not answering," she said to David, with a worried look on her face.

Old habits die hard. Perhaps she is dead, thought David, but all he said to Jessica was, "She most likely forgot to turn her phone on."

"You're probably right. Do you think that I should drive into town, just in case? I might see her somewhere," Jessica fretted. "It is getting late most of the shops are closed."

"I would give it another half an hour and then try calling her again," David advised.

"Ok," said Jessica, returning to her task of getting supper ready.

Half an hour was almost up and even David was beginning to think his mother in law had died under a car, when almost on cue the telephone rang. Jessica bounded over to the phone way too fast to act unconcerned. "Mother where have you been it's almost quarter to seven," she said.

A little demon inside of David wished it were someone else on the other end of the receiver, sadly no.

"I told you I had to go into the town, I had some business to sort out," said Allison. "I am just calling to let you know that I will be late for supper. I am going to get a taxi back to the house."

"Well you should have rung earlier," Jessica admonished, "You have had us worried sick."

Well one of us has, thought David.

"I will tell you all about it when I get back," was the only explanation Jessica's mother offered.

"Where are you? David will come and pick you up," Jessica said, as David rolled his eyes towards the ceiling.

"Right in the town centre by the monument," she answered. David was dutifully despatched, any protestations would have been in vain.

David got back in the car and was just pulling out of the driveway when it started to pour down with rain. He put the windscreen wipers on, turned on the radio and nudged the dial for the car heater up a notch. There is nothing more satisfying than sat in your car, cosy and warm, listening to music as you watch the rest of the world get drenched he thought to himself. If anybody had been with him in the car at that moment they would have seen a look on his face that could only be described as pure smugness.

Jessica's mother was sheltering in a shop doorway. David annoyed all of the other cars behind him by suddenly pulling over to the kerb when he spotted her. He realised that he would have to get out of the car to help his mother in law. On any other day he might have let her struggle but she had her crutches and several small shopping bags to contend with and even David could not be that callous. He opened his car door and got a wet blast in the face that wiped the look of smug contentment straight off his face. He put Allison's shopping, and the crutches, in the back of the car and helped her into the passenger seat, all of the while feeling the cold icy drips of water roll down the back of his neck. Finally they drove off.

"We were really worried about you, we wondered what had happened to you," he kept up the pretence of caring. Allison said nothing, she looked lost in thought, or maybe she was just glad to be out of the rain. "Jessica has cooked us lasagne for tea," David continued.

"That's nice, dear," she said, and for a moment David wondered if she might thank him for coming out in the pouring rain to pick her up. That would be a miracle. "I have been thinking..." she let her voice trail off.

She knew David would have to ask. "Thinking what?"

"Well it has been a few years now since Jessica's father passed away and I am not getting any younger," said Allison.

"Nonsense you are as young as you feel," David felt obliged to say.

"Well be that as it may and what with all of this hospital business, I have been thinking about life in general." Allison continued.

Where on earth is this going, thought David, although he was not sure he would like the answer, "That's nice," was all he could bring himself to say.

"Anyway maybe it is time I stopped rattling around my old Victorian house in Acton, with all of its memories and everything, perhaps it's time for me to sell up so I can move closer to my family."

David tried to think of something to say, something, anything, anything at all, but the only words that came out of his mouth were, "Bloody Hell!"

They drove the rest of the way home in silence, luckily for David they were almost there.

Chapter Nineteen

By the time Thursday had arrived with still no word from Ronald, speculation in the office ran rife. Normally the first thing everyone asked when somebody never showed up was the obligatory, "Do you think he is dead," but strangely enough everybody was too scared to ask it. Whether it was a matter of prescience or whether it was so close to the forefront of everyone's mind that nobody dared ask, who could say? By now every one of them was genuinely concerned. Andrew had tried Ronald's number several times in vain, and it had hit that point of no return where the only option left open to him was to phone the police, or the hospital.

"I will make that call," said Andrew, to an office staff who stared at him as though he had just confessed to a murder. What else could he do?

Nobody in the office had ever worked harder, and not just because they feared for their jobs. It felt like as long as they worked hard, and buried their heads in the sand, Ronnie would come strolling in with a cheesy grin on his face and a story to tell. They all pretended to be disinterested as they listened with all of their might to the one sided conversation Andrew was having with the very nice police officer. Andrew passed on all of the details of Ronald's name and address and assured the officer that to the best of his knowledge the contact details Ronald had given were accurate. Andrew thanked the police telephone operator for his time and asked if they could inform him if there was any news, and then hung up.

"I have let the police know what has happened," Andrew said to the office in general. As if there was a single one of them who did not know. "They said they would get back to me if there are any further developments."

Time went by and then more time went by, David began to feel like that if the day went any slower it would start going backwards. Shortly before Hell froze over, quarter past three earth time, a uniformed officer arrived at the office and asked to speak to a Mr Andrew Jones. David felt his buttocks clench like never before and he was almost nauseous with trepidation. "Is there somewhere quiet we can have a word," said the policeman.

"Yes, surely," replied Andrew, "we can step outside into the corridor."

A whole twenty minutes went by and everybody stared at each other as they waited for any news as the sound of muffled speech drifted into the office.

"What do you think has happened," whispered Felicity to David.

"I don't know, but it doesn't sound good," David whispered back.

After a while Andrew thanked the officer for his time and stepped back into an office where the staff had never looked busier. He looked ashen. "Umm I am sorry to interrupt your work," he said, "but I have just received some news which I am afraid is rather unfortunate." They all knew what was coming. "I regret to have to tell you that our friend and colleague Ronald Atkinson sadly has passed away."

"What happened?" said Adam and Eric almost in unison.

"Well details are a bit sketchy but the police broke in to his home and found a body which they believe had suffered a heart attack."

There it was the death knell, the sound David had feared, final and absolute confirmation that Ronald had died. He tried telling himself it had to be true but the words just echoed around his brain, lies bouncing off the inside of his head looking for somewhere to settle and become reality. Visibly shaken the office went unnervingly quiet, perhaps they were mourning the death of their friend, or perhaps they were lamenting their own mortality.

Ever the gentleman Andrew told the group, "I think under the circumstances we can allow you all to leave a little bit earlier today."

How fucking magnanimous, thought David, but perhaps he was just venting his anger and frustration at Andrew over the situation. Ronald's desk had suddenly turned into a mausoleum, David stole quick glances at it and then quickly had to look away in case Ronald spotted him. Curiously enough he noticed that the others were the same, almost as if to even look in that direction felt disrespectful.

Some days are better than others, David continued his surmising of the whole situation, this day has got to be the worst. Occasionally he would make eye contact with one of the other members of his team and then look away in shame, as though even to show friendliness to another human being was a bad thing to do right now.

"So if you want to pack your things, you can go now," said Andrew, "David can I ask you to stay behind a moment."

The others filed out of the office eager to leave the funeral parlour that had once been their place of work, until there was only David and Andrew left staring at each other.

"I know that this has been a difficult day for you, David," said Andrew to his colleague, "but we must face up to the practicalities of the situation. Ronald is dead and he is not coming back and, hard as it may seem, somebody is going to have to go through his desk, and all of his work itinerary, to sort it out." David tried to protest but Andrew was on a roll, "And I don't think we can afford to be tardy on this matter, because the longer we take to get around to it the more stress it is going to put on the rest of the staff."

"But are you sure that this is the right time to be discussing these matters, Andrew," said David, "After all we have only just found out that the man is dead."

Andrew would have none of it, "Now is definitely the right time, David, we must strike while the iron is hot," an analogy that David saw as completely incongruous, "it is a matter of urgency that we get it done as soon as possible." Then Andrew paused and said, "You don't have to do it now, first thing in the morning would be fine."

David's mind was in turmoil, "What me...you want me to do it...in the morning?"

"Yes, of course," Andrew replied," perhaps you could come in early to get it done before the others get here, cause them less concern."

David's blood was starting to boil, the man was fucking unbelievable, he started to tell Andrew how he felt, "Andrew, I can't..."

"Nonsense, David, it has to be done and it has to be you," Andrew cut him off in his tracks. "You are the right man for the job, you are the only one I can trust to get it right." It was way too late for compliments, David was seething inside. Andrew looked at David and smiled, which at that moment was totally the wrong thing to do, "Don't you see, David, in many ways this is turning out to be a good thing."

"How on earth could you possibly think that Ronald dying is a good thing?" said David, too gobsmacked to hide any of the sarcasm in his voice.

"Well it is obvious," said Andrew, oblivious to David's darkening tones, "Now at least I don't have to decide which member of the team to let go, the choice has been made for me."

David hit him.

Blood was running down Andrew's face. "I am putting this in the staff accident report book," Andrew shouted after David who was storming out of the door.

"I don't care," David shouted back.

Chapter Twenty

There is an unwritten cosmic law in the universe that if you are having the worst day of your life, everybody has to jump on the bandwagon. When David eventually got home after nightmare tailbacks caused by roadworks on Cardrew Avenue , Jessica was in the kitchen waiting for him arms folded, definitely not happy. "Mother said that when she told you about wanting to sell her house and move closer, you swore at her," she accused.

"I did not swear at her," David tried to defend himself, "I just accidentally swore."

"Oh well that makes it alright then, does it David," said Jessica, "As long as you were swearing in general, and not at anyone in particular, that makes it fine."

"What does it matter that was ages ago, that was on Monday, a lot has happened since then."

"So you don't deny it then. How would you like me to go around and swear at your parents?"

"Now you are just being ridiculous."

"I am the one being ridiculous. Do you think that it is ok to upset my mother when all she wants to do is be nearer to us because she cares about us?"

"She cares about you, maybe," said David being more than a little petulant.

"Well I think that you owe her an apology," said Jessica angrily.

"Look," said David, "I have got more things on my mind than your stupid mother."

"So now she is stupid as well is she, David?"

"No I didn't mean that," said David, sensing that the whole argument was slipping away from him. "I just meant..."

"Well I don't care what you meant, until you apologise you can cook your own tea."

"Jessica, I need to tell you something," said David. Jessica pretended not to be listening. "I hit Andrew in the face."

"There you go again, David," stormed Jessica, truly livid now, "always exaggerating, always making a mountain out of a molehill. Why can't you just be honest and straightforward?"

"I did I hit Andrew in the face." It sounded lame even to David. "He had a nosebleed and everything."

"Alright suppose I did believe you," said Jessica, "Why did you hit Andrew in the face, David?"

"Because Ronald is dead."

"Let me get this straight, you hit Andrew in the face because Ronald is dead."

"Yes." David knew that it would never stand up in court.

"And you think that is normal, do you?" Jessica accused.

"No, but what you have to understand is..."

"I don't have to understand anything, David. I am starting to wonder if I am married to a man or a monster."

"Jessica, please listen to me..."

"I am not listening to anything, anymore, I am going out." Jessica stormed out into the hall, grabbed her coat, fumbled around for her car keys and then was gone.

David felt that this day could not get any worse. He decided that more than anything he needed a drink and headed for the kitchen cupboard. At the back of the cupboard there was a bottle of whisky and David went for gold. The first glass burned his throat but boy did it feel good, so he poured himself another. After a while David sat in the kitchen in the semi-darkness sipping his drink and feeling completely maudlin.

There is a second cosmic law in the universe that states that when your life has gone completely to pot help will come from the most unexpected source. The kitchen door opened and in walked Allison, mother in law from Hell.

"I forgot you were still here," said David, "Have you come to gloat?" It was the liquor talking.

"No," said Allison, "I thought I might join you for a drink."

"Well you can't, you're not allowed, not with your medication."

Allison got a glass out of the dishwasher and poured herself a stiff drink, "Well," she said, "I don't think a small one is going to do any harm. Medicinal purposes only."

They sat for a while side by side old adversaries contemplating their lot. How did it end up like this, where did we go wrong? "The answer is not there in the bottle, you know," Allison informed David.

"Probably not but it feels good right now," David responded.

"What have you got to worry about, you have got a lovely wife and family, people who love you?"

"My friend died." David cut her short.

"Well boo hoo," Allison mimicked, "Do you think it was easy for me when my Bill died, I didn't think I had the strength to carry on but somehow I dusted myself down. I got up and I carried on so can you."

"I have probably lost my job, and my wife has gone off to God knows where, Allison, at the moment I am not in the mood." David admonished.

"There you go again, poor me, always the victim. As you know David you and I have not always seen eye to eye..."

"Ain't that the truth," David confirmed.

"But..." Allison chose to ignore his derisory remarks, "Over the years I have come to realise that you are a good husband, and a decent father, and Jessica could have done a heck of a lot worse. You have always worked hard and provided a decent home, and there are plenty of men out there who are a complete waste of space."

Compliments from the old battle-axe, David wondered if he was dreaming. "I suppose like any decent parents you were just worried about your only daughter," he offered as a crumb of compensation.

"So if you think I am going to stand by and watch as you throw it all away you've got another thought coming," Here was the real Allison, the old battle-axe returning. "You need to get on that phone find out where my daughter is and if necessary get on your bended knees and beg for forgiveness."

"I've been trying, she won't answer," David whined pitifully.

"Well in that case, you had better get on the phone and ask your boss for your old job back."

"I can't I hit him in the face."

"Did you have good reason?"

"Yeah he thought my workmate dying was a good thing."

Allison laughed, "It probably was a spur of the moment thing, I am sure he will get over it in the morning."

David laughed, "Do you know underneath that tough exterior there is a decent person trying to get out."

"Yes," said Allison, "and underneath that wimpy shell there is a real man just hiding away."

"I hate you," said David, but this time he was not being serious.

"I hate you too," said Allison light-heartedly, "That is why I have to move closer to keep an eye on what you are up to."

Maybe it was the alcohol or maybe the heat of the moment but David broke a lifetimes worth of bitterness and kissed his mother in law on the cheek. Neither of them had spotted that during the latter part of their exchange Jessica had come back and slipped through the front door unnoticed. Through the open kitchen door she could see her husband, father of her two children, and her mother, the woman who helped raise her, getting along. It was simply too much for any woman to take and she fainted.

Chapter Twenty-One

The next day David decided not to go to work, partly because of all of the events from the day before but mostly because he had the largest hangover ever. He put off calling in as long as he could but eventually he could leave it no more. He hoped and prayed he would not have to speak to Andrew. The switchboard operator told him to wait one moment and put him straight through to Andrew.

"Hello, Andrew Smith," said a familiar voice, although slightly nasally, maybe David had broken his nose.

"Hi Andrew it's me, David."

"Oh."

"I am phoning up to apologise for my outrageous behaviour yesterday, and I want to say I am really, really, really sorry."

"You do realise that assaulting another member of staff is a serious matter," said Andrew.

"Yes, I just lost control of myself, all of this business with Ronald dying has really upset me." Eating humble pie was difficult at the best of times, with a hangover even worse.

"Well, David, under the circumstances, I am going to be lenient and give you the benefit of the doubt." Inside his head David he could only hear the words, 'Thank God'. "But I warn you," said Andrew, "if it ever happens again, I am going straight to Dixon without a moment's hesitation."

David suspected that he would never hear the end of it for months on end, if not the rest of his working life, but his eleventh hour reprieve was certainly enough for the time being. "Once again Andrew I just want to say how truly sorry I am. You and I have always been friends," he lied, "and I, honest to goodness, just don't know what came over me."

Andrew's tone softened slightly, "Look David, I know these are difficult times for everybody so take the day off, get your thoughts together, and come in tomorrow and we will say no more about it."

"Thanks Andrew," David wanted to say more but was worried anything else would sound mushy and trite.

"That's ok," said Andrew, and they hung up.

Things were on the up, Jessica came over and kissed him, "Did you manage to sort things out with Andrew?" she asked.

"You're kidding, with my charm." David smiled, "And how are you this beautiful morning Mrs Banks, the woman I love, mother of my children?"

"I am a lot better," she answered.

"Don't ever do that to me again you gave me the fright of my life, and your mother." He was, of course, referring to Jessica's fainting episode.

"I think it was the shock of seeing both of you behaving like friends," she said.

As if by magic Jessica's mother appeared, how did she get such perfect timing, did she wait just outside the stage door, "How is my favourite daughter and son in law?" she asked.

Favourite only because we are her only daughter and son in law, thought David. Trying to let go of over twenty years of feuding was going to be difficult. "Actually Allison, I feel good enough to take you ladies shopping today, you can help Jessica choose some clothes to take to Cornwall, and I won't even moan about the credit card bill." He suddenly had a pang of guilt that he should not be feeling happy when Ronald had just died but he knew that he had to move on.

Jessica's eyes lit up, "Well I do need to get some clothes for a summer wardrobe," she said, "and it would be nice to have a second opinion, mother."

"Agreed," said Allison.

"You don't have to come, David," Jessica continued, "I know that you hate shopping, I can drive into town and pick the kids up on the way home."

From Hell to Paradise in under twenty-four hours. "In that case," said David, "I am going over to see my mum and dad. I have been a bit worried about them since the fire."

Everyone in harmonious agreement they each started preparing to go their separate ways.

It took David almost two hours to reach Middlesex, but before he knew it he was parked outside of his mum and dad's house. This is going to be a one heck of a surprise for them, he thought, and then in a moment of panic he suddenly realised that perhaps before driving all of that way, he might have done well to telephone them first to let them know he was coming. They have got to be in, they must be, they never go anywhere but the doubts were there as he pressed the familiar doorbell. It took a while and a lot of baited breath but eventually his mother answered.

"David," exclaimed his mother, "Is that really you?"

"Yes it is, mum."

"Where are Jessica and the children?"

"Jessica has gone shopping with her mum, and the kids are in school," David answered.

"What are you doing here?" his mum asked, and then with a look of consternation added, "Has something happened?"

"Nothing's happened mum, I just wanted to come and see you."

"Ok."

"Well aren't you going to invite me in?" David asked with a grin on his face.

His mother regained her composure, "Yes, of course, come in. Your father is out the back he will be delighted to see you."

David followed her through the house. "So this is the new kitchen I have been hearing about," he said, "They have done a marvellous job." David looked around the shiny new kitchen, pulling knobs and opening cupboards.

"I must admit we are very pleased it is far better than the old one," his mother agreed, and then added, "Dad is in the garden, go out and see him. I will put the kettle on."

David did as he was told, sometimes it feels like you never grow up. "Hi dad," he shouted across to the shadowy figure watering the garden. David looked at him and for a moment completely choked up as he remembered what happened to Ronald.

"By God it's David." David's father took everything in his stride, if they announced imminent nuclear war he would probably just say, "Well that is a bit of a rum do."

"I was worried about you," said David, "What happened with the fire? What the Hell have you done to your arm?" David's father had his arm in a cast.

"Oh that, I fell off the ladder when I was painting the ceiling."

David let it ride, "Have you heard from Colin or Peter?"

"Ah I think your mother was going to say something about that," was his dad's cryptic reply.

"About what?"

"Never mind, can you turn the hose off for me, there's a good fellow." Once again junior David did as he was told.

They heard a shout from the kitchen, "Tea is ready, shall I bring it out?"

"No we will come in," his dad shouted back.

David sipped his over-sweetened tea, he had given up sugar years ago but he did not have the heart to tell his parents. His mother grilled him all about Jessica and the children until he got to the point where he wondered if the interrogation would ever stop, but eventually he found chance to say, "Are Colin and Peter ok?" David did not like the way that his parents gave each other sideways glances as he asked the question.

"I am sure Peter and Wendy will be fine, it's just a blip that's all. I mean all marriages have their ups and downs," his mum answered.

"What are you talking about?"

"The affair Wendy was having with the chap where she used to work, it's over now, everything is sorted."

"Pete told me she had a new job, now I know why." David shook his head in disbelief, and sipped some more tea. "Anyway, at least Colin is alright." That look again. "Colin is alright, isn't he?"

"He and Emma are very happy," said his mum. That was her name Emma, David could never remember it. "After all nobody could have seen the Spanish crash coming. They may have lost the house, and heck of a lot of their savings, but at least they have got each other. Colin is a good architect I am sure he will get another job soon."

David wondered at what point he left the known universe and stepped into the twilight zone. "But this is terrible, why didn't you tell me?"

"Well you know how much you worry, David."

David needed to bring some semblance of normality back into his life, "Mum, dad, is there anything else I should know before my world totally collapses?"

"No everything else is just fine, honestly," replied his mum, "Well, apart from your dad's cancer scare and that was a complete false alarm. The doctor said that once his arm gets better he will be one hundred percent."

"And the main thing is that your mum is ok too," said his father, "We can get a new car but we can't replace her can we," he added, winking at his wife and slapping her on the bottom.

David could hardly take it all in, "You've had an accident, mum?"

"Oh you don't have to fret, David, mostly it was just the bonnet and the one of the wings. "The police were very good they said it could have happened to anybody."

"What did you do?" he meant the crash.

"The accelerator pedal jammed and I hit a wall," his mum answered, as though she were describing baking a cake to the women's guild. "I was very lucky, if it had happened a minute or two later I would never have missed that bus."

"Oh that's fine then," said David sarcastically, and then a thought occurred to him, "Does Jessica know any of this?"

"We thought it best not to tell her because she has had a lot on her mind with her mum, lately." There is one small consolation in this madness, thought David.

After a while, dazed and more than little confused, David made his farewells and kissed his parents goodbye, with strict instructions that if anything more happened they were to phone him or Jessica immediately. "And that includes any news from Colin or Peter," he added.

Driving away from disaster world and back towards normality David longed for his holiday in Cornwall more than he could ever have imagined.

Chapter Twenty-Two

It was uneasy at first but after a few days David and Andrew were back on track, and it was almost like their contretemps had never happened. Somebody, during his absence, had cleared away Ronald's desk (probably Felicity) and the furniture had been moved in such a way as to imply that no-one had ever been there. In a strange way David was glad that it had been done and it irked him even more than probably Andrew had been right all along.

Days passed and then one afternoon Andrew got the phone call that they had all been expecting. "I have just been talking to Ronald's son," Andrew informed the office, "And Ronald's funeral is next Tuesday in St Michael's church at ten o'clock. Everyone can have the day off but I expect you all to be there." With the last remark he looked directly at Adam. Adam shrugged his shoulders and pulled a face that said 'what me'. "Afterwards we are all invited to The Queens Arms where there will be sandwiches," said Andrew, disregarding Adam's look .

The following Tuesday was a grey and dismal day, suitable really, David surmised as he stared out of the passenger window of the car. He had thought it best to let Jessica do the driving. As they drove past the cemetery on the way to the chapel, David spotted the hotel that Harry had been going on about. "Oh look, there is that hotel where Harry and Jane's daughter are having their reception," he pointed out to Jessica.

Jessica tried her hardest to look at the hotels exterior and drive at the same time, she narrowly missed a pot-hole. "Looks very up market," she exclaimed.

"The Park Regent Hotel," David read the sign out loud, "I bet it must have cost Harry and Jane a fortune."

Within minutes they had arrived at their destination. "There doesn't seem to be many people here," David stated the blatantly obvious.

"Perhaps there are more inside," said Jessica.

After a fashion various members of the office team showed up. First there was Andrew and his wife, shortly followed by Eric and Lolita, who had given Adam a lift, and then finally in her mini came Felicity all by herself. They gathered outside the church where a couple of old men had assembled and a younger looking fellow who on questioning turned out to be Ronald's son. David was appalled by the fact that Ronald's ex-wife and his other son were not attending the funeral. The hearse arrived and from nowhere so did the vicar and they all went in.

The vicar spoke a little about Ronald's life, and they all sang some hymns and then one of the old gentlemen talked about how he liked to go fishing with Ronald. "I never knew he liked fishing," David whispered to Jessica.

David wondered if Ronald's son might speak but it did not seem to be the case. "May I say something?" asked Andrew to the vicar.

The vicar stepped aside, "Of course," he said.

"Ronald was an esteemed colleague and a very hard worker, he was a well respected older member of our team at Harman and Cooke, and as such will be sorely missed." Andrew eulogized to an almost empty church.

David was starting to see red, where were those Harman and Cooke Directors who used to call themselves Ronald's friends, and all of those people who hung out with him when he had money, and where the bloody Hell were the rest of his family. David stood up, "I would like to say something too," he almost shouted. Everyone looked. David went to the front, climbed up on the pulpit, and stared at all of the faces. "Yes he was an 'esteemed colleague', he almost mimicked Andrew, "but he was also our friend. Not many people know this about Ronald but he had a terrific sense of humour, he was a great guy and if I get to achieve half of the things in my lifetime that he has done I shall be a very happy man." From nowhere David started to cry, "Goodbye Ronnie," he blubbed, "I shall miss you very much." He stood there bawling his eyes out in front of a stunned audience, until Jessica jumped up and led him by the hand back to his seat.

104

For David the rest of the ceremony was a blur and he did not stop crying right up until they put Ronald's coffin into the ground, and they all went off to the pub.

Everyone approached David with caution, Felicity was the first to brave it over, drink in hand. "Are you alright?" she asked nervously.

"I am better now," David tried to smile.

Eric and Lolita followed timidly, their eyes said it all. "Congratulations on your good news," said Jessica to the pair. At least someone managed to keep it together, thought David and he loved her so much that he almost started to cry again.

A relieved looking Andrew thought it safe to venture over with his wife, "You're not going to hit me," he joked.

"No not today, Andrew," David produced a teary-eyed laugh.

They all looked awkward. "Where's Adam?" asked Felicity.

"Well he can't have gone far," Eric answered, "We gave him a lift."

On further inspection Adam was spotted on the other side of the bar chatting up the barmaid.

"What happened to that girl he was dating," said Felicity, "What was her name again...Cadenza, that was it."

"Maybe she stopped laughing," David felt compelled to say, all humour had not left him in his sadness.

"Well she isn't going to like him chatting up barmaids at funerals." Felicity surmised.

"Or indeed at any other event," David added, he could feel his old self returning.

"Adam come over here," Andrew shouted across to the boy.

Adam sauntered over, "Alright," he said to the group in general.

"Does Cadenza know you are flirting with the bar staff," Felicity asked accusingly.

"I wasn't flirting," Adam defended, "I was just asking her name, that's all. Besides me and Caddy are taking it easy at the moment."

How fickle is loves young heart, thought David, only a short while ago Cadenza was the one, now she was relegated to the second division, and soon, if previous experience was anything to go, by she would disappear off of the radar altogether.

Tentatively, for fear of upsetting David again, they talked a little bit about Ronald, raised a glass in his honour, and then one by one bade their farewells to Ronald's son, and soon they were all gone. Under Jessica's instructions David had been warned not to say anything to Ronald's son because, as she put it, "You can't blame him, at least he had the decency to turn up."

Driving back home David stared out of the car window. Jessica knew him well enough to keep quiet.

Chapter Twenty-Three

Over the coming weeks having reached what can only be described as his nadir of sadness, things just got better and better for David. The children were getting used to the idea of going to Cornwall, Lucy had primed all of her friends not to be surprised if they hear of a tragic drowning off of the Cornish coast, and Simon having done some research on the place, fuelled on by some of his teachers, wanted to look at some of the old tin mines and sea-faring heritage. As the days got closer Jessica kept herself busy crossing everything off of her check list. David for his part made sure that the car was booked in for a service and that the tyres were safe.

If there was any sadness in their joyous anticipation of two weeks in the West Country it was from a direction David could have never anticipated . Having scanned every available house for sale within a twenty mile radius of their home Jessica's mum hit them with the shock announcement that she wanted to return to her own place. Normally this would have sent David into axioms of joy but he found himself disheartened at the thought of Allison going back to her house. He would miss the old girl.

"Is there nothing we can do to convince you to stay?" David asked Jessica's mum, and this time he had the conviction of someone who meant it.

"I've looked and there isn't a property for miles that comes anywhere near what I have got now," Allison replied, "Besides I miss my place it has got all of my memories of Bill, and of Jessica's childhood, and don't forget my friends are there, and the ladies of the Bridge club."

David was not sure if by implication the 'ladies of the Bridge club' were not considered friends. He looked at Jessica and could see the tears already welling up in her eyes. Thinking fast he went for the reassurance technique, "You know that we will come and visit you all of the time," he offered, "and you can come here and stay as much and as often as you like." Judging by the softening of the trembling lips on Jessica's face he might have scored gold.

"Are you sure this is what you want, mum?" Jessica asked, "The children will miss their gran, so much." Inside his head David substituted the word 'children' for the word 'Jessica'.

"Well my leg is a lot better and I have one or two bills to sort out, and even though the Davenports have been keeping an eye on the place, I do worry that anything can happen while I am not there. I can always move house at a later date, who knows, something really good might come onto the market."

The latter statement seemed to appease Jessica's growing distress, "If we can't change your mind," she said, "let us know when you want to go back and we will take you home."

Plans were made, bags were packed and with a car more laden than that of a mountaineer who was about to climb Everest, David found himself waving goodbye to his mother in law as Jessica drove her away. Exit stage left. As usual the children were nowhere to be seen, having said their goodbyes the night before and earned their reward from granny's purse.

With some time on his hands before Jessica got back David decided to make a couple of phone calls. First of all he phoned mark just to give him an update on the latest plans for their Cornish adventure. Mark had been delighted when David had told him about booking the holiday cottage and seemed to get more and more excited as the time drew near. "I have borrowed a couple of surf boards and you might fit into one of my wetsuits, so I can teach you how to ride the waves," he said to David.

The whole idea of 'riding the waves' filled David with abject horror. "Won't that be great," said David, trying to hide is concern.

"Jess is about the same size as Hannah so she can come too."

"I am sure she will love it," David lied.

"How's the mother in law, still giving you a hard time?" Mark was blissfully unaware of the latest developments in David's and Allison's relationship.

"Oddly enough Jessica is taking her back to her house right now even as we speak."

108

"God, you must be delighted."

"Actually I think I might miss the old girl in a strange way."

"You really do need that holiday, David," was all Mark could think to say.

They chatted some more about a few of the delights that Cornwall had to offer, the best place to get a meal, where not to go in the summer, beautiful coastal sunsets, and before long David found himself longing to go right away. He made is goodbyes to Mark and sat in his armchair listening to the noise of the world outside. He knew that he had been putting off the inevitable but the time had come to make the phone call he did not want to make.

The phone had hardly made the third ring when a familiar voice answered, "Hello, Colin Banks."

"Colin it's me Davey," David's speech was still in Mark mode.

"David!" Colin exclaimed, "What a surprise."

"Mum told me what happened with your job and the house and everything, are you ok?"

"Well bearing up under the strain, you know what it is like." David did not know what it was like. "Emma has managed to get a job in the local tapas bar so we are getting by."

"That's nice," David thought that his voice could not have sounded more condescending if he tried.

"And with a bit of luck I have got a couple of leads that might get me some more work."

David was always impressed that Colin could put a positive spin on almost anything, a trait that he got from mum and dad. If Colin had been on the Titanic he would have probably pointed out that they had a free bar. "Mum and dad have had a few problems of their own," David confessed, he did not mean to say anything but it sort of came out.

"Oh yeah, what's that?" asked Colin.

"Well dad broke his arm and mum had a car crash."

"Are they ok, how did it happen?"

David realised that Colin was unaware of the events in their parents household, and wished that he had never said anything. "Oh it's nothing," David was becoming more like his parents every day, "Mum caught her foot on the accelerator and hit a wall, she's fine."

"She must have hit the wall pretty damn hard for dad to break his arm," said Colin the inquisitor.

"No dad broke his arm when he fell off the ladder, he wasn't in the car."

"Oh well thank Christ for that," said Colin sarcastically, "That makes it ok."

David completely understood Colin's reaction and probably would have responded in exactly the same way if the roles were reversed. He tried to reassure Colin, "Honestly Colin they are fine, I went to see them the other day." David did not dare to mention the cancer scare.

Colin let it drop, he probably had enough problems of his own to deal with. "Have you heard from Peter and Wendy?" he asked.

David's heart went into his mouth, he knew there was a reason he had not wanted to make this phone call. How much did Colin know, was he testing him to see if he would tell the truth? "Pete and Wendy are good," David squeaked, "As far as I know."

"And you and Jessica are ok?" asked Colin, "Didn't you say that you are going down to Cornwall?"

The moment had passed, David felt relieved that the conversation was back on safe waters. "Yeah, I am taking the whole family, we are staying in this lovely converted barn not too far from the coast."

They talked about holiday plans, and Mark, and how Cornwall was beautiful during the summer, and how David really must make the effort to get over to Spain one year, and then suddenly the telephone call was over. David said goodbye, wished Emma well, and hung up the receiver. It could have been a lot worse, he thought to himself, as he reflected on their conversation. Time to make a cup of coffee.

Chapter Twenty-Four

Life at the office was getting better too. The shock of losing Ronald had passed and it was not long before they were back to their old ways of insulting one another and wishing for better things. And then there was the morning when Adam came in with a black eye.

"What the Hell has happened to you?" David was the first to spot his colleague's misfortune.

"I met this girl and I don't think that her boyfriend was too happy with me talking to her." Adam explained.

"Was he a big guy?" Eric asked.

"No, I could have had him," said Adam, with false bravado. Everyone knew it was a lie.

"So why didn't you?" Eric came back with a sneer.

"I'd had a couple of pints and was feeling a bit drunk, besides she wasn't worth it."

Her not being worth it was a plausible enough reason in Eric's world. "You want to watch yourself, Adam, next time you might get hurt. You had better learn yourself karate or something." As he said it Eric pretended to spar with Adam.

"Leave him alone," said Felicity, light heartedly, "Anyway he could probably have you, Eric, any day of the week."

"I would like to see him try," Eric responded.

"Adam, may I have a word," Andrew pitched in. They stood to one side and most of the office could hear Andrew telling Adam that coming to work with a black eye showed a complete lack of professionalism, and what if Graeme Dixon should walk in etc. Adam for his part showed complete indifference.

Not so for Eric, whether it was because he saw himself as Adam's mentor, or whether he was indignant over the injustice of it all, or who knows for whatever reason Eric decided to throw his hat into the crowd. "I think you are being a little harsh on young Adam there,

Andrew," he said, "Surely it is not his fault if some idiot gives him a shiner."

You could have heard a pin drop. "I am in charge here, Eric, and I will thank you to get on with your work and mind your own business." Andrew said with some conviction.

Clash of the Titans, or at least handbags at dawn. "As I recall, Andrew, it was not so long ago you had suffered a facial injury yourself, what if Graeme Dixon had walked in then." Being a potential father had obviously toughened Eric up. David did not like where this was going on two levels, firstly any kind of conflict in the workplace was uncomfortable at best, unbearable at worst, and secondly the obvious reference too David's act of violence and the memories it could stir up.

"That was different," said Andrew.

"In what way?" questioned Eric.

Andrew tried to exert his authority, "When you run this office Eric, and you have been doing it as long as I have, you will learn that there are certain rules and regulations that must be adhered to."

"Bollocks," retorted Eric, "Everyone knows I could run this place far better than you can." Right at that moment 'everyone' squirmed with embarrassment, and tried to look as though they were so engrossed in their work that they hardly noticed there was an argument going on.

"Be that as it may," Andrew refused to back down, for which David had to give him some respect, "You are not the person in charge here and as far as I am concerned you never will be, so go back to your work," his voice was getting louder, "and do as you are told."

A camera on the wall would have seen Adam's, Felicity's and David's dumbstruck faces. Eric stood there looking Andrew in the face weighing his options. Eventually the seriousness of oncoming fatherhood must have kicked in, because with much banging of office implements and a lot of huffing and puffing Eric went back to his computer screen. "You haven't heard the last of this," he had to say as a parting shot.

Andrew looked around the office, red in the face, "Now," he said out loud to the room in general, "Unless there is anyone else here who thinks that they can do my job for me, would you all get on with your work." All of the mice did as they were told.

After the longest day ever, and there had been some pretty long ones lately, David could hardly wait to get home and tell Jessica all about it. "No really," he told her, "It was pretty bad."

Jessica could tell from the excitement in his voice that this time David was not exaggerating, "And all because Adam came in with a black eye," she said.

"Yeah, this fatherhood thing must be really affecting Eric."

"You were just the same when Lucy was born," said Jessica.

"I wasn't that bad."

"Yes you were, you nearly knocked out that bloke because he bumped into me when I was pregnant."

"He was drunk."

"No he wasn't."

"Well he looked drunk."

Just at that moment the object David tried so hard to protect all those fifteen years ago stomped her way into the kitchen. "Hi Lucy, did you have a nice day at school?" David asked. It was a stupid question because Lucy never had a nice day at school. School was a place where her wicked and twisted parents sent their only daughter to torment her.

"That Miss Parkinson, she is so 'trick' she is backwards, she doesn't know anything about history," Lucy declared.

That must be why she got herself a degree in the subject and decided to become a history teacher, thought David. "Why's that?" were the words that came out of his mouth.

"She has never heard of Dracula, Lord Byron or Mary Shelley, or anything. What does she know about history? She is making us do homework on the Crimean War." Definitely the crime of the century.

"I think you are mixing up your history lessons with English Literature," suggested Jessica, hopefully.

"That is even worse," Lucy decried, "Mr Edmunson doesn't know anything about anything. Do you know we have to read Jane Austin." The bastard.

David went for a different approach, "School breaks up in a couple of weeks, are you looking forward to it?"

"Mum, dad can Jack come to Cornwall with us?" Lucy responded.

"I am afraid not," replied David, destroyer of worlds, "We have already booked up, and besides I want this to be a family holiday, all of us together."

Jessica looked poised to bang her judge's gavel, but instead Lucy just muttered the word, "Ok."

No tantrums, no storming out of the kitchen, not even a raised voice, maybe our daughter is on drugs was all David could think. "So you are happy with that," he blurted.

"Yeah I guess so." When did their tempestuous daughter leave and get replaced by the darling young angel they used to know and love?

David tried to offer some morsels of comfort, "When we get to Cornwall, you can stay up late every night, and if you are really lucky we might even let you have a drink or two," he said, with a wink and a smile. Jessica looked at him reproachfully.

"Thanks dad," she said. Now David was really worried that Lucy was on drugs, but for the first time in his life he said nothing. Truly this was a day of unpredictability.

Chapter Twenty-Five

All wounds heal, even pride, and like the discolouration around Adam's eye, the tension between Eric and Andrew began to dissipate over a period of time. If anything there was a new found respect between Andrew and Eric which David found most disconcerting. David had always been Andrew's unwritten second-in-command and inside he felt almost threatened by this new state of affairs.

But the world keeps on turning and it was not long before David's sojourn down to Cornwall was no longer a blip on the horizon but an imminent arrival. The children had already broken up from school and it was only a matter of days before David was to take his annual two weeks leave and set off for pastures new.

The car had been serviced and two of the tyres replaced, and with much inhaling of the breathe David had parted with his hard earned cash to pay for the deed. Jessica, for her part, had worried herself stupid and packed every item that she thought they might need for the next two weeks, from hairspray to insect repellent and everything else in between. She had drawn up an itinerary of things to do and what clothes to pack, but eventually had reached the point where she could do no more and started to relax. The children had packed away most of their bedrooms and then under Jessica's supervision had reduced it to a level where it would not take three Sherpa's and several pack mules to carry it all. Eventually they opted for their computer tablets, mobile phones and favourite items of clothing.

Within a short period of time all of the goodbyes had been made at the office and well wishes offered, and David unexpectedly was driving home the night before the holiday. He pulled into the petrol station and filled the car up until it would not take one last drop of fuel. It felt good, there is something about a full tank that gives a man a warm glow inside When he arrived home David opened the front door, and was surprised to see that Jessica had filled the hallway with all manner of objects. Everything else had been squeezed into several suitcases, and it felt like the eve of battle.

"Mother had sent us another cheque for a thousand pounds," said Jessica excitedly, "So now we don't have to worry about spending money for the holiday at all."

"Are you sure that we can accept it," David enquired, "After all she has given us so much already."

"I called her and she is adamant that we have to take it. She says that if we don't spend it she will be most annoyed and that this is our special holiday and we have to accept the money," said Jessica.

David had already drawn over a thousand out of the bank and his wallet was bulging. Feeling good turned into feeling better, damn it, he felt like Rockerfeller, and with a beautiful wife to boot, could a man feel any happier? One last call to Mark and they would be ready to go in the morning.

The morning came and the whole Banks family were running around the house preparing for the off. The bathroom was a constant source of irritation for the next person who was waiting to use it. David loaded the car while Jessica frantically cleaned around him, so that, in her words, "the house will be lovely and tidy when we get back." Harry and Jane next door and been left a set of keys and given instructions to keep an eye on the place as well as the numbers to call if there was a problem. The children bickered with each other and soon enough there was nothing else to do but go. Firmly ensconced in their overloaded car and with one last look at the house David turned the ignition and the family Banks set off for Cornwall.

At the end of the drive the sat-nav told David to turn right when he knew full well that he had to turn left. I am supposed to trust this thing to take me all of the way down to the West Country, David thought to himself. Meanwhile, barely ten miles down the road, the children were already starting to fight with each other. 'He said this', 'she said that', they complained to their mother as though she had not been in the front seat of the car and heard every word they were saying. "For goodness sake, shut up," Jessica admonished, "or we will never get there." David could not quite see the correlation

116

between there arguing and them never getting there but he drove on regardless.

Road followed road and before they knew it they were on the M5 motorway and headed towards their destination, David opted to pull into the next service station so that he could brace himself for the major part of the journey and give the children one last chance to use the toilet facilities. "Are you sure you don't want to go?" he asked Simon for the umpteenth time.

"Yes, dad I'm fine," the boy replied.

"There won't be a second chance on the motorway," David stressed the point.

"Honestly dad, I'm fine," Simon repeated.

One last slurp of their drinks and the Banks family were back in the car and on their way. A few miles down the road David was a bit concerned to hear the lady traffic announcer on the radio warning of some tailbacks on the M5 but like all holidaymakers he drove on regardless. It was not long before they found themselves in a queue of cars which had ground almost completely to a halt.

After a few hours of being stuck on the motorway the vehicle you are travelling in can become less of a mode of transport and more of a coffin. Whose bloody idea was it to go to Cornwall anyway, David thought to himself knowing all along that it had been his. The children's arguments had turned into all out war, and Jessica resigned herself to staring out of the passenger window as the hedges crept by an inch at a time. From his hearse David looked across the barrier to the other side of the motorway at all of the free-moving traffic and wished he was with them. "There is a nine mile traffic jam on the M5 because of an accident," the traffic announcer came back to say, "try to avoid the area if you can." David wondered if he was in Hell.

"Dad I'm busting," Simon whined, "Is there a toilet around here?"

It took forever, and David could hear the sound of Hell freezing all around him, but eventually they were at the front of the queue of cars at the spot where the accident had taken place. The area was strewn with debris from the crash and there were at least three crumpled cars that David could see, and police cars everywhere. The Banks family stared with both shock and awe at the whole scene as they slowly passed by, imagining what it was like for the people involved. "Somebody's holiday has been absolutely ruined, I bet," said David, while thinking thank God it was not ours.

And then freedom, the open road beckoned towards them and at last they were on their way.

"Dad I really must use the bathroom," Simon wailed, in considerable pain now.

"Oh for Fuck's sake," said David, out loud and then regretted it as Jessica slapped him on the arm. "Just hold on five more minutes, Simon, I think there is a service station up ahead."

Chapter Twenty-Six

It was getting late in the evening when they finally reached their destination and despite a few difficult negotiations with some very narrow country lanes the sat-nav had done its job and taken them to the door. Both Lucy and Simon were fast asleep in the back seat of the car and Jessica woke up from her trance as they got nearer.

The enclave of converted barns looked idyllic from the outside, and were reminiscent of the rustic cottages you see on picture postcards. David was quite impressed, "Do you know, they look even better in real life than they do in the pictures," he said to Jessica, who had to agree. They drove past the barns and up to the nearby farmhouse as they had been instructed by telephone to get the keys. David knocked on the farm door and was a little concerned when he heard the sound of dogs barking on the other side. The door was opened by a rosy faced amiable looking woman and David seriously started to wonder if he was in a nineteen thirties advertising commercial. "Mr and Mrs Banks," he said to the woman, and wondered why he sounded so formal.

"Oh you're the couple in barn five," said the woman, in between telling the dogs to keep quiet. "Don't mind the dogs they will settle down in a minute." David thought that the only thing that would settle the dogs down would be the taste of human flesh. "I will just grab the keys and I will meet you down there."

David and Jessica got back in the car where they felt safe from the savage hounds and drove back to the complex of barns. There were other cars parked in the courtyard area but no-one to be seen. They spotted a door with a brass number 'five' on it and waited in the parking space outside. True to her word the farmer's wife appeared, keys in hand, and not a dog in sight. David and Jessica left the children asleep in the back of the car and followed the woman into the converted barn.

If they thought that the outside of the building was impressive it was nothing to the picture perfect interior. There was a large living room with cottage style beams and a rustic looking wood burner which then led on to an equally impressive kitchen with range style cooking facilities and a huge wooden table. "I will just show you the how to turn on the hot water," said the farmer's wife, oblivious to David and Jessica's dumbfounded faces. She ran through where different electrical sockets and light switches were, and other information she thought they needed to know, and then bade them to follow her upstairs where she showed them a beautiful bathroom with an ornamental tub and the three bedrooms. Before long she bid them farewell and left strict instructions that if there were any problems they were to call her immediately, and then was gone.

David looked at Jessica, and Jessica looked at David, and then they both looked at each other, and burst out laughing. "It's wonderful," said David, wiping the tears from his eyes.

"I love it," Jessica agreed, "Did you see the bathroom?"

David had seen the bathroom, "And the kitchen," he said.

"Oh David I love it. Can we live here?"

"Only if you divorce me and marry a millionaire."

They started to explore their new domain, "On the coffee table was a bottle of wine, some chocolates and a large bunch of flowers with a note saying, 'Welcome to Kernick farm Cottages. We hope that you enjoy your stay here'. There was also a local newspaper, some magazines on Cornwall and lots of advertising leaflets on places to go and things to do in the area. Thoughtfully the owners had put tea and coffee in the cupboards and in the fridge some milk, eggs, butter and a fresh loaf of bread.

After much prodding and poking about the place they decided that they would wake the children and show them their new found utopia. "Lucy, Simon wake up," David lightly shook the children awake, "Come and see the cottage it is amazing." Sleepily the children shook themselves awake and followed their dad into the building. They were completely underwhelmed.

"Is this it?" asked Simon.

"Where's my room?" asked Lucy racing upstairs with barely a glance at the living room or kitchen.

Too tired to do anything else David and Jessica decided that they would go shopping in the morning to get some food and maybe try to get the feel of the area they were staying in. David got out his mobile to let Mark know they had arrived and to make plans to meet up the later on the next day. Mark could barely contain his excitement, "You will love little Zak he is such a tearaway," he said, jokingly, "He has his little hands into everything." David thought that Mark was going to get in his car and drive over to the cottages there and then, but he knew him to be more considerate.

Jessica helped the children to set up camp in their new temporary bedrooms, and then came back downstairs to share a glass of wine with David. She snuggled up to David on the sofa and they worked their way through some of the leaflets and the periodicals. "There are all sorts of things we can do while we are down here," she let David know, "There is Tintagel, Lands End, St. Michael's Mount, Eden Project, Jamaica Inn, the list is endless."

"I quite fancy St Ives we could visit the Tate art gallery there." Along with his new formality David had developed a sudden interest in art, Cornwall was obviously already having an effect on him. "Shall we get the stuff in from the car?" he asked Jessica, suddenly remembering the overloaded vehicle.

"Let's just leave it until the morning," Jessica replied, it seemed Cornwall was having its effect upon her too.

Later that evening they set off for the luxurious bedroom, "Real beams!" David exclaimed. There was a window overlooking the courtyard at the front of the building and a skylight which looked over the green fields at the back. "Do you hear that?" he asked Jessica.

"What?" Jessica answered.

"That's just it not a sound, no cars, no noise, no nothing."

Fuelled by their excitement, and not just a little by the alcohol, before long their feelings towards each other became more and more amorous, until they could contain themselves no more. Afterwards they lay in bed in the semi-darkness listening to the noises of the countryside. A little later they heard a car pull up, unable to curtail his curiosity David peered through the curtains. "It must be the people staying in one of the other barns," he let Jessica know, stating the blatantly obvious, "There is a couple getting out of the car." Sherlock Holmes had nothing on David Banks. He watched the couple until they disappeared from his line of vision and then he went back to bed.

It had been a long day and the whole Banks family slept the sleep of princesses and kings, apart from David who dreamt of car crashes.

Chapter Twenty-Seven

The first thing David heard in the morning was a cockerel crowing, he had never heard one before, only in movies, and was taken aback as to how loud they were in real life. Jessica was already awake and sat up in bed taking in her new surroundings, "Did you sleep well?" she asked him.

"Apart from the fact that I dreamt that we were all trapped in a car crash," he answered, "I guess that accident we saw on the motorway must have affected me more than I thought."

"Never mind you are here now, safe and sound," said Jessica, reaching over and giving him a kiss.

The children were already up and sat downstairs, one eye on their tablet computers and the other on the television in the background. "Hi mum, hi dad," said Simon. "What's for breakfast?"

Lucy waved an offhand wave, she had so much to tell all of her friends on Facebook that they would probably go into overload.

"I will do you some toast and me and your dad are going shopping later," Jessica answered Simon's question.

"Cool," he said.

Breakfast complete, David decided that the time had come to unload the car "Lucy, Simon, can you give me a hand to bring the stuff in, please?" he asked them, in a way that was more of an order than a question. For a second or two they thought about protesting and then thought better of it. Outside David could see a group of young lads emerging from one of the other buildings who he presumed were surfers as they had some surf boards strapped to the roof of their vehicle and wet suits everywhere. They were laughing and joking as they went in and out of their cottage, probably getting ready to go to the beach. David felt uncomfortable with the attention they were getting from Lucy, and it disheartened him to think that she was at an age where she was discovering boys.

Safely back inside the house Jessica set about putting everything in its place and David called Mark, yet again, to arrange a time to meet up later and to get directions for the sat-nav. "Where is the nearest supermarket?" he asked, towards the end of their conversation, "We need to get some food and things for the stay." Having got his answer it was not long before David and Jessica set off for the nearest out of town store a few miles away, leaving the children back at base with strict instructions not to touch anything or go anywhere.

Usually David hated shopping but this was different this was holiday shopping. It being a different store added to the novelty, and Jessica's frustration, and David delighted in filling up the trolley with things Jessica would normally never approve of. He overloaded the trolley with cakes and ice creams and all manner of unhealthy snacks, and when they got to the beer aisle David knocked himself out with several cans and even a couple bottles of expensive wine. On another day Jessica would have told him to put it all back, but not today, today they were on holiday, when David saw the price of the bill he almost wished she had.

After a light lunch of sandwiches and fizzy drinks they all jumped in the car to head over to see Mark, Hannah and Zak. The skies were cloudy but at least it was not raining.

From the outside the house that Mark was renting was a lot smaller than expected, it was an end of terrace granite building. "Number 43, this must be the place," said David. There was a small patch of garden at the front of the building which looked completely overgrown bar for the concrete path leading up to the door. They had barely stepped out of the car when the front door flew open and an over eager Mark came racing out to meet them, small boy in his arms.

Davey, Jess welcome to sunny Cornwall," he greeted them, "You will love it here. This is Zak...and you must be Lucy," Thank God he got the name right, thought David, "And this young man, must be Simon, my haven't you grown." Mark kissed Jessica on the cheek and gave David such a hug that David worried they were going to kill the child caught between them. "Come in, come in." Mark beckoned them inside the house.

Although it looked small from the outside the building was surprisingly deceptive and went back quite a long way. Hannah was in the kitchen at the far end of the house, like the building she was a deceptively pretty girl hidden underneath a plain exterior, although David would never admit that to Jessica. "Would anyone like a cup of tea?" Hannah asked.

"Yes, please," David answered for all of them. The children settled for juice.

"Follow me," said Mark, too impatient to wait for the kettle to boil.

Mark gave them a guided tour of the house and quizzed them on their thoughts of the West Country so far. Tour over the Banks family made a fuss of the cute looking baby and waited for their drinks. It was not long before Lucy and Simon became restless, there was a long elongated garden out the back which was in less of an unkempt condition that the one at the front and the children set out to explore, taking the toddler with them. David wondered if he should warn them not to hurt the infant but he left it to his better judgement. The four adults sat around the galley kitchen drinking their brews and reminiscing about times long forgotten. The beauty of a true friendship is that when you meet up after a long period of time it is like the years just melt away and it feels as if you had never parted. Mark and David laughed and joked with each other about old times, and even Jessica had drawn Hannah out of her shell. Soon the two women disappeared off to look at some hand-crafted quilt covers Hannah had bought in a local market.

The afternoon flew past but before long the children were back in the house and the toddler, having been made such a fuss of, was crying for food, or for something. Mark tried to convince them to stay for dinner but they politely refused not wishing to overstay their welcome but only on the condition that they return the next day for a barbecue. David added his own condition that Mark must bring his family to see the fabulous barn they were staying in. All agreed, and the Banks family set off for base camp.

Driving back David took the executive decision of detouring off to look at the coast, and from the vantage point of a cliff-top lay-by they took in the breathtaking views of the ocean. The whole family were stunned into silence. David looked at Simon and wondered if he had ever seen the sea before. On the way back they drove through a small coastal town and David was delighted to spot a chip shop, "Oh we must," he said to Jessica who did not put up any kind of resistance. They sat outside the shop on some wooden benches, staring out to sea, eating their fish and chips. With his stomach full and feeling really complacent, David breathed in the salty sea air and thought that he had found Paradise.

Chapter Twenty-Eight

The next day David awoke to the familiar sound of the bird crowing, "It's bloody half past six in the morning," he complained to no-one in particular as Jessica was still fast asleep. It takes time for city dwellers to adapt to the noise of the country, so David lay in bed listening to Jessica snore and the rural world getting ready for a new day. It got to the point where he could stand it no more and had decided to get up when he fell back asleep. When he awoke for the second time Jessica was already up and gone downstairs, David looked at the little portable alarm clock and was surprised to see that it had gone ten.

Showered and refreshed David went downstairs and checked the weather, hazy sunshine. It was not quite hot enough for the beach so, after much infighting, it was decided that they would go and visit the Eden project.

When you have seen one dome, you have seen them all, David thought to himself as they wandered around the site looking at the pretty plants and flowers. Surprisingly the other three loved it, even Lucy, David played along with their enthusiasm. "I wish we had a greenhouse back home," Lucy enthused.

David knew that she would be bored of it within a week and the plants would die inside their glass prison. "Maybe we should get a few house plants when we get back," he offered, "Start with a couple of cactus plants or something." David was reluctant to stifle any interest Lucy showed in anything that was not morbid, it being such a rare occurrence.

Simon read the little signs which explained some of the plants to the visitors, with keen interest, "Did you know that this plant is found mainly in Peru and can grow to a height of over twenty metres," he read. They had all read the placards for themselves but they acted as though they had not.

David pretended to be astonished, "Really twenty metres," he said, while wishing they had left the thing in Peru where it belonged. Some people, in this world, just do not have green fingers, David was one of them. The day passed pleasantly enough but secretly David was glad when they got back to the barns.

"Can we go again, some time?" Lucy asked.

"Maybe," David answered, and inside his head he uttered the words, 'but not in my lifetime'.

By the time they got over to Mark and Hannah's place David's mood had significantly improved. Jessica had offered to drive so he knew that he could enjoy a few drinks, and the weather had brightened up considerably. The smell of the meat wafting out from the rear garden was almost tortuous it made David so hungry.

Mark looked up from culinary delights, "Hi," he said, "Perfect timing."

"We brought a few cans of beer with us," said David," And a bottle of wine. I don't know what sort of wine it is but it must be good because it was bloody expensive." Everyone laughed.

"The best type," said Mark with a cheesy grin.

The food was delicious, and the wine lived up to its expensive price tag. David held true to his prior commitment and even let the children have a glass of beer, all be it that Simon's glass was three quarters lemonade. They sat on plastic garden chairs around a plastic table, and laughed and joked and made the most of what was turning out to be a fine summers evening.

"I never did ask you what it is that you do for a living these days?" David enquired of Mark.

"Well mostly I help design websites for start up businesses," he answered, "There is not a great deal of work but I can do it from home, and it gives me chance to enjoy my beautiful son, here, and my lovely girlfriend." Those feelings of envy started creeping in again but Mark was such a nice guy that David knew he deserved it, and, after everything he had been through with his ex-wife, Mark deserved a lottery win to boot. David had always wondered what it was he had seen in his ex-wife to begin with, but he guessed opposites attract, in this case polar opposites. Hannah was a far better woman in so many ways.

The night was a great success and the icing on the cake was when they had finished talking about their day at the Eden project, Mark leaned over to David and whispered in his ear, "I don't see what they see in the place myself." If David had not been surrounded by witnesses he might have kissed Mark there and then and not through any sort of latent homosexual tendencies.

"There is something I can still show you," said Mark, arousing David's curiosity, "Follow me."

David followed Mark to the bottom of the elongated garden where there was an old tumbledown looking garage and a couple of sheds. Mark took David inside one of the sheds and he was taken aback by what he saw inside. The inside of the building had been lined with what looked like tin foil and there was a large ultra-bright light shining down onto what looked like a dozen marijuana plants. The smell was overpowering.

"What do you think," asked mark with a wry smile on his face. David and Mark had experimented with cannabis during their formative years, but David had assumed that, like him, Mark had given up smoking the stuff many years ago.

"Bloody Hell, Mark," David exclaimed, "Does your landlord know you are growing dope at the bottom of your garden?"

"I damn well hope so," said Mark laughing, "He was the one who gave me the seeds."

"Oh!"

"We share the buds half each...I don't sell it or nothing," Mark added defensively.

"Right,"

"Come on David, you have to try some, I have some already dried in a tin," said Mark.

David must have been more drunk than he thought because he agreed. They went back to the plastic table and from nowhere Mark produced a tin full of the dried green herb and proceeded to roll a joint, all the while being mindful not to let the elder children see what he was doing. Jessica frowned but did not say anything, she knew that Mark and David had smoked the stuff in their younger days but she had never participated herself. Mark lit the reefer and inhaled a few long drags and passed it over to David, it tasted better than David remembered but it still made him cough. He got used to it, and after a few more puffs David opted to pass the joint back to Mark, who for his part passed it over to Hannah. It was not long before the joint was back in David's mouth again and he was taking in the herbal mixture. At first everything seemed fine and David with his heightened sense of awareness thought everything to be hysterically funny, but how quickly it turned and the next thing David knew the outside world was spinning uncontrollably. He tried to stand up but his legs had gone from under him and then a toxic combination of the beer, the narcotic and the food it all became too much for him and suddenly he was vomiting everywhere.

At least Mark could see the funny side, "I think that I may have made that joint a little too strong for you," he laughed.

"It feels like I have been hit by a train," said David, feeling slightly better having been sick.

"I think that this might be our cue to go home," said Jessica, "Let me take him away before he does any more damage to the place." Lucy and Simon were inside the house, so she called for them to get ready to go.

Lucy was the first to appear, "What is wrong with dad?" she asked.

"I think that your father has had a little too much to drink," Jessica answered.

The next thing he knew David was inside car, or the snugly spaceship as he preferred to think of it, belted up on the passenger seat and Jessica was driving them all home. He tried to remember if he had said goodnight to Mark or Hannah but his head was so fuzzy he could not recollect a thing. David did not know when or how they got back to the cottage, all he knew was that this new bed was the most comfortable thing under God's creation. Very soon David had drifted off into slumber and slept like he had never slept before.

Chapter Twenty-Nine

Even the cockerel crowing could not wake David the following day. When he did finally get up, all be it with a thumping head, he was delighted to see that it was a beautiful blue sunny day. He half expected Jessica to give him a lecture but she did not say anything to him. "I don't think that I will be doing that again," he said to her as she came out of the bathroom, as if to put a cap on the matter.

"Right, children," David declared once they had all finished breakfast, "We are going to the beach today and no arguments." There were no arguments, so after a while they were in the car heading towards the coast, with everything Jessica thought they would need in the back of the vehicle.

When they got there David was shocked at the car park charges, but faced with the alternative of turning around and going back to the barn he reluctantly paid it. They all bundled out of the car, bags, blankets and towels akimbo and set off for the sandy shore. Jessica insisted that they buy a wind-break from a nearby shop so David did as he was told.

They trundled across the hot sand dragging their clobber with them until they found a suitable slot where they could set up camp for the day. David looked around him at all the tanned handsome young men and beautiful maidens, and wondered if this were the beach where every top model took a vacation. He was suddenly painfully aware of his white slightly pot-bellied appearance and was glad that Jessica had made him buy the windbreak so that he could hide slightly behind it. Lucy and Simon set off to explore.

The sun was glorious and as the day went on it became blisteringly hot. David felt comforted by the fact that other equally out of shape people, if not worse, had joined them on the beach. After a fashion Lucy and Simon came back so David jumped up and declared, "Come on you lot let's go in the water."

The plan was to run into the sea and dive straight in but as the first waves touched David's feet the plan went right out the window. The water was freezing, not just cold but sub-zero in David's mind. Lucy and Simon kept going wading into the ocean, "Come on dad," they shouted. Timidly David inched his way deeper and deeper into the ocean until the water was above his knees. He did not like the look of some of the waves heading towards him either, one such wave took the water level up to his waist an experience David did not like. It took a while, and some playful splashing from Lucy and Simon, but before long David was swimming about in the shallow water. He actually quite enjoyed it once his body had adapted to its new arctic surroundings. His mouth tasted of salt and he felt a sense of euphoria.

When he started to shudder David knew it was time to go back to Jessica. Surprisingly the edge of the ocean where the shallow waves lapped against the shore felt warm beneath David's feet on the way out of the water. When they got back to the windbreak David took delight in shaking some of the water clinging to his body over Jessica and she responded by playfully hitting him with the book she was reading. "Well the sharks didn't get us today," David joked.

"Are there sharks in the water," asked Simon gleefully.

"Only if your mother goes in," David responded, to which Jessica hit him with her book again.

The day was exceptionally hot and by unanimous consent David was despatched to get ice creams for everyone. He feigned discontent but secretly was eager to have an excuse to get one for himself. The cornets of ice cream had started to melt by the time he got back to his family but everyone loved them, especially the flakes David had opted for as extras.

Time passed and David relished the sun as he lay across the sand covered blanket soaking up the rays, he felt like he was in a dream. "Put some more sunscreen on David you are starting to burn," Jessica admonished.

"I am fine," he said.

"Well if you think you know best," was all Jessica could say.

Let's go and explore," David said to Lucy and Simon, one who was sunbathing and the other who was building sandcastles. They were both up for it so the dad and the two children headed off towards the rocky area at the side of the bay, but not before Jessica had made all three of them put tee-shirts on for fear of sunburn. Once around the corner and slightly out of sight of the beach they were amazed to discover caves and rock pools and all manner of things to explore. Further on was another sandy beach with nobody on it, "A secluded beach," David exclaimed, feeling like Livingstone, "We have to tell your mother." They day wore on and the children were getting tired and whiney, so they all three headed back to where they had come from. "I don't remember the sea being this close to the shore," said David, feeling a little bit concerned.

When they got to the rocks that they had traversed so readily earlier on in the day, it soon became apparent that the waves were breaking over them and forward momentum was going to be difficult, and then horror of horrors there was a deep gully that had not seemed to be there before blocking their way entirely. "Let's go back to that secluded beach and see if there is path leading out from there," said David, now beginning to get really worried.

The secluded beach was nearly completely underwater and with gnawing anxiety David realised that they were trapped on the rocks. "How long before the tide goes out?" David asked out loud to himself, mainly, because he knew the children would not have the answer.

"Were stuck on the rocks, aren't we dad," said Lucy, "We're going to drown."

"Are we going to drown, dad?" Simon asked forlornly and looked like he was about to cry.

"Nobody is going to drown," David felt like he had to take control of the situation. He looked upwards in the vain hope that they might be able to climb the cliff above them and instantly dismissed that idea. "We just have to wait for the tide to go out a little." The tide did not seem to be going anywhere apart from further in. "Did either of you bring your mobile phones, I think we should call your mother," said David, or the coastguard he secretly thought. Neither had brought their phones with them.

The sun was dipping in the late afternoon sky and the three of them sat on the rocks worrying about their imminent future. The silence was palpable. From nowhere a boat appeared and seemed to be heading their way, it was a large rubber dinghy with a small crew and an outboard motor, on the side of the vessel were the letters 'RNLI'. David did not mean to, but he started waving his arms frantically at the craft and never felt more stupid in all of his life. The boat neared and one of the crew signalled for them to try to get to what was left of the secluded beach. The boat pulled up as near as it could to the shore and a man waded up to meet them, inside David wondered if drowning would have been less embarrassing. "Mr Banks?" their rescuer enquired, as if there were plenty of other stranded fathers with two children dotted about the place.

"'I am afraid so," David answered, his words sounding as stupid as he felt. They were all given lifejackets and helped into the raft, one at a time. "How did you find us?" David shouted above the roar of the boats engine.

"Your wife was worried about you and called the coastguard," their hero answered, "Also you were spotted by some footpath walkers. They were taken back to the shore of the beach they had left what now felt like many years ago, where to add to their humiliation in front of several onlookers they were given a brief medical examination. To add to his woes Jessica was there too and David thought that she looked like she had been crying. David promised to donate so much money to the RNLI that in the future he might become their patron, hands were shaken, belated warnings given about the dangers of the Cornish coast, rip currents and unexpected tides and they all parted company. Jessica grabbed Simon and Lucy and gave David such a look he thought about calling the lifeboat men back and asking if they would take him back to the rocks where they had just come from.

Later that night as David lay in bed tossing and turning, while burning alive from the excessive sunburn, all Jessica could say was, "Serves you right."

Chapter Thirty

All Mark could do was laugh when David told him about his fiasco on the rocks the day before. "Everyone knows that the tides can turn on a sixpence round here," he said.

"Everyone who lives here," said David, and then in a mock Cornish accent added, "Not us 'ere city folk."

They had invited Mark's family over to look at the barn, and Jessica had rustled up a lovely salad which they had all enjoyed, and for dessert some shop bought chocolate torte. The sparkling white wine Mark had contributed to the mix only added to their enjoyment.

The Banks family had spent the day visiting several local tourist attractions and trying out the famous Cornish pasties. They had thought it best to stay away from the beaches after yesterday's debacle and also they were still suffering from the after effects of the sunburn, well, some of them.

"I hope this hasn't put you off going surfing," Mark added.

David did not need anything extra to put him off going surfing, "Of course not," he lied.

"Ok, when?" asked Mark.

David frantically searched inside his head for excuses not to surf and could find none, "Umm..."

"Come on Davey, it will be great, I can get Hannah's friend to look after Zak and we can all go together," Mark could not contain himself, "I can borrow a couple of boards and we have got some spare wetsuits that should fit you and Jessica..."

"Wait a minute," said Jessica, "I never said I was going."

"Oh but you must, mustn't she Hannah?"

Hannah agreed, "Once you get the hang of it, you will love it," she said.

"You may have to buy a couple of suits for Lucy and Simon and maybe a couple of body boards but they are cheap enough in the local supermarket," Mark would not be deterred, "I can't do it tomorrow because we will have to arrange a babysitter, so how about the day after?"

Reluctantly David agreed, all the while feeling like King Louis XVI setting a date for the guillotine. "Weather permitting," he added.

"Of course," Mark agreed.

Arrangements were made and the then it was done, no going back now for the Banks family they were committed .

The following day was hard for David and Jessica to really enjoy. They had a lovely day looking at St Michael's Mount, and a delicious cream tea followed by a jaunt down to Lands End, but there was only one thing foremost on both of their minds. "Why did you have to rope me into it?" Jessica asked petulantly, "You know I don't like the water at the best of times."

"Well you should have said something," David parried. It felt as though by taking chunks out of each other they could distract from what was really on their minds this infernal surfing debacle.

The children were quite excited by the prospect and relished in choosing wet suits and body boards for the next days entertainment. David wondered if the real joy was in watching their parents drown as they became future orphans.

Another restless nights sleep followed by the interminable rooster crowing and the new day was upon them. The weather conspired against them too, by being mostly bright sunshine with a few hazy spells, perfect surfing weather. From nowhere Mark appeared in a huge white transit van loaded to the nines with surf boards, wet suits and other equipment. "Look what I have managed to borrow," he said, barely able to contain his excitement about the van.

"Yay," David could barely hide his sarcasm.

David and Jessica loaded the van with extra stuff, and then they all clambered aboard squeezing themselves into all sorts of unfortunate places, and then they were off. Mark took them to a reasonably quiet beach on the North coast, popular with surfers, "This is the place," he said, stating the blatantly obvious.

David noticed that the same group of lads who were staying in one of the cottages next to theirs were also at the same beach. Now I am one of them, he thought, the ignominy of it all not entirely lost on

136

him. They parked up and Lucy went over to speak to their blonde haired leader, "Hi Thom," she said.

"How the Hell does she know his name," David whispered to Jessica.

"I don't know," Jessica responded.

Lucy laughed and joked with the young surfers while David seethed inside, but before long he had too much going on trying to get into his wetsuit, to worry about what other people were up to. With Mark and Hannah's help they were finally all suited up and they all carried their boards to the sand beside the waves. Foremost on David's mind was the size of the boards they looked much bigger than in the movies, he thought. "Mark made them place the boards on the sand and went through basic instructions on what to do. He showed them how to mount the board and gave them elementary surf school for beginners. "When you are riding the waves towards somebody, the acceptable thing to do is to drop out of the wave so that you don't collide," he told them. David thought that he was speaking Martian. "Has anybody got any questions?" Mark asked, "If not let's head off for the water.

When they were in the water, which seemed mercifully less cold because of the wetsuits, Mark and Hannah showed them how to ride the back of the board and push the front under the broken waves so that they could get out to where the waves were breaking. From the shore the waves looked no more than ripples on a duck filled pond, and yet from the perspective of being in the ocean in David's mind each one was a mini tsunami waiting to claim a life. Mark got his board to where the waves were breaking and suddenly looked like a participant in a Beach Boys video riding it towards the shore. Meanwhile David was having the Devil's own job just getting his board out to sea, to where the waves were breaking, every time he felt that he was going forward the waves seemed to be pushing him back. David looked back at the shore, a place he now sorely missed, and when he turned around there was a huge wave almost upon him. Suddenly David and the board went flying tumbling and twirling in the oceans spray, and just at the point where he was certain he had to breathe water he found himself deposited at his beloved shoreline.

Undeterred David staunchly got back on his board and set out to sea once again.

With Hannah's help Jessica got the hang of surfing almost straight away. "You're a natural," said Hannah. In a parallel universe there was probably another David who was quite delighted for her, this one was not. The children were doing well with their body boards too, it seemed like there was only one person not doing great. With gritty determination that person tried his level best to get his board to a place where he could ride a wave towards the shore. One wave went under him and David was glad that it had not taken him with it, sadly not so for the next wave, once again David found himself spinning helplessly in a maelstrom of white water, fighting for air. "I will fucking get to ride a bloody wave," David shouted above the roar of the ocean, whilst shaking his fist at God the only person who could possibly hear his cries.

Mark appeared from nowhere, paddling up beside David, "How are you doing?" he shouted over.

"If I can just get the board to where the waves are breaking I think I can do it," David answered.

"Follow me," said Mark.

Together David and Mark set off from the shallow water, Mark slightly ahead. A wave came, a big wave, it just went under Mark's board and then broke right on top of David. The board went flying off into the air and its leash which was attached by Velcro to David's leg ripped off. Having parted company with his board David went crashing to the oceans floor and knocked himself senseless. David spluttered helplessly and swallowed water and suspected he was going to die, somehow he struggled back to the beach.

Mark was very kind, and having retrieved David's board for him told him to take some time out. They sat on the beach together pontificating about life. Soaking up the sun and watching the rest of his family having fun rejuvenated David, together with some pre-prepared snacks and refreshments, and before long he felt brave enough to get back into the ocean. Mark did some emergency repairs to the board's leash, and the pair were ready to go.

With Mark by his side this time David got to the break point, and with just a little encouragement was for at least three seconds riding a wave, after which David found himself spitting ocean floor once again. Forget dropping out of someone's wave, if anybody had been in his flight path they surely would have collided, joining David in white water misery. David did not care he was in ecstasy, he was in Heaven, he had ruled the waves, for one brief moment in time, and then a curious thing happened to David, he felt really alive for the first time in his life. Mark had been right to force them to give surfing a go, David realised, it was probably the reason they had stayed such good friends for years, Mark's ability to drag David into pastures new, and although David knew he would probably never attempt surfing ever again in his life he was glad to have tried it once, and loved Mark for it.

The rest of the day was just perfect, even though David never got to ride a second wave, and the whole Banks family were shattered when they eventually got back to base. They all slept well that night, and in the morning nobody heard the cockerel crowing, perhaps the bird simply gave up knowing it was a losing battle.

Chapter Thirty-One

The rest of the holiday melted into a blur of excitement and adventure for David and the rest of the family. They looked at abandoned old tin mines, visited seaside towns and in general visited all the local tourist attractions in the area. One night David even took Jessica out for a meal in a fancy restaurant and only griped for a short while when he saw the bill.

But like the passing of a book's pages, in the words of the old adage time waits for no man, and before long their two weeks in Cornwall were drawing to a close.

Mark could not hide his despondency at the thought of David and Jessica taking their family back home. "We made a special farewell cake for you," he said, "And look, Zak did some of the icing."

The icing looked a terrible mess but David did not care and he thought that it was the most beautiful cake he had ever seen. Choking back the tears, he managed to say, "It's lovely, thank you," and then quickly quipped, "You haven't put any of that funny stuff in it," to hide his embarrassment.

Farewells were made, small gifts exchanged and they all promised each other that they would stay in touch via the telephone and the internet. Vague promises were made that they should try to do it all again next year, and before they knew it they were all waving goodbye and blowing kisses to each other.

Lucy and Simon were going to miss Cornwall too. Lucy had befriended their surfer neighbours and had formed a special bond with the golden haired Thomas. At any other time David would have hated this but somehow the magic of the West Country, or maybe it was the near death surfing experience, had mellowed him, and he was happy to see his daughter genuinely happy for the first time in ages. When Lucy was hanging out with the surfers Simon had strung along and as such he was adopted by the group, who affectionately called him 'Dweeb'. They were all going to miss each other, surfers and children alike.

"Do you think one day when we retire that we can buy a cottage just like this one?" asked Jessica, as she frantically set about tidying the place in preparation for handing the keys back.

David kissed her on the cheek, "My love, I will buy you an even bigger, better cottage than this one with ocean views and we can keep chickens in the yard, and play with the grandchildren."

"And can we drink wine on the porch as the sun goes down?" Jessica asked.

"Gallons of the stuff," David added, "The neighbours will think that we are alcoholics."

"Sounds perfect," said Jessica, as they embraced each other in the kitchen, and David knew that this memory would stay with him for a long time if not the rest of his life.

They loaded the car with all of their belongings, and had the extra problem of trying to fit in all of the presents they had bought for their friends and family back home. David decided to face the friendly farmer's wife, and her hounds of the Baskervilles, one last time so that he could give the keys back, and they were ready to go. Lucy and Simon had disappeared but David and Jessica had no trouble finding them, they went over to surf cottage, "We have to go now," said David.

"Please dad, just one more minute," pleaded Lucy.

"Ok, we will wait in the car but only one more minute," David granted.

Five minutes later Lucy and Simon appeared and meandered their way over to the vehicle. David tried not to let the fact that Lucy and Thom were blowing kisses to each other irk him. Remember it is just a fad, he kept saying to himself over and over again inside his head.

The sat-nav was set to home and they pulled out of the driveway waving goodbye to the holiday cottages forever. "Stop the car," said Jessica.

"Why?" asked David, worried that maybe she had forgotten something.

"We haven't got any photos of us standing outside the cottages," she replied.

David turned the car around and much to the bemusement of the watching surfer group, who probably wondered what the Hell was going on, they all went back and stood in front of what had become 'their' cottage. Thom did the honours of taking the snapshots.

On the second attempt they succeeded in leaving properly. David drove to the nearest petrol station and put in a full tank of fuel and they were off.

As the car passed over the bridge that crossed the River Tamar, they knew that they had left Cornwall behind for Devon and that they were headed home. Everyone agreed that for them life would never be the same again, and that they would never go back to their old ways. Everyone knew it was a lie.

6051615R00082

Printed in Great Britain
by Amazon.co.uk, Ltd.,
Marston Gate.